Ravens on a Wire

Also by Andrew Bacevich

Ravens on a Wire

A Novel

Andrew Bacevich

For Barrye, Rick, Dan, Marc, Russ, and Jeff,
With warm memories of our days in Fulda

The author expresses his gratitude to friends who generously commented on preliminary drafts of this book. They include Nancy Bacevich, Casey Brower, Steve Brown, Rob Goff, Bob Ivany, Lawrence Kaplan, Jane Wheeler, and Scott Wheeler.

He would also like to thank Stewart Berg and Falling Marbles Press for their professionalism and efficiency in preparing the manuscript for publication.

FALLING MARBLES PRESS
Marble Falls, Texas
www.fallingmarbles.com

"Cascading Worth, One Work at a Time"

THE KINGDOM OF THE RAVENS, 1976

East Germany

Czechoslovakia

1/16

2/16

Bamberg

Bindlach

16

3/16

Nürnberg

Amberg

L

Camp Rötz

West Germany

Contents

Ravens on a Wire

Prologue

Quickdraw 6 is annoyed. More than annoyed—he is flat-out pissed.

A carefully scripted visit meant to impress General Aloysius "Big Al" Paterson, Chief of Staff of the whole U.S. Army, is falling apart, and there is nothing he can do about it.

As 60th Colonel of the 16th Armored Cavalry Regiment, ever since the Civil War proudly known as the Ravens—cavalry units take their heritage seriously—Barton Caldwell ought to be a near shoe-in for promotion to brigadier general, the goal he has worked toward ever since pinning on the bars of a second lieutenant, some twenty years before. This visit was supposed to seal the deal. The fact that they are headed to a border encampment where a young Black captain is in charge offers a nice extra touch. After the eruptions of racial animosity that swept through the Army's ranks beginning in the 1960s, equal opportunity has become a top priority. Caldwell wants Big Al to know that his regiment has gotten the message. Here, then, is one corner of the

Army committed to eradicating the afflictions induced by Vietnam.

Now, a goddamn jeep accident near the Czech border has fucked everything up. The initial reports coming into the ROC from Blackbird 47, an aero-scout dispatched to the scene and hovering above the accident site, are not good. A jeep flipped over at the bottom of a ravine. Soldiers seriously hurt, perhaps worse. No direct contact with anyone on the ground.

Eavesdropping on the regimental command frequency, Caldwell had pieced together a picture of the scene from its fragments of information. So, too, had his guest, sitting opposite and wearing an identical headset. The picture was not a pretty one. Recovering troops and equipment was now becoming the priority, but the glacial weather and difficult terrain meant that recovery would pose additional risks. The bad situation was likely to get worse before it got better.

Since assuming command as Lord of the Ravens, Caldwell, a youthful forty-one, had conducted dozens of these heliborne show-and-tell border tours, all of them uneventful. Exuding confidence, combined with Southern folksiness that he could turn on like a light switch, while flashing the Rolex on his wrist, he had a knack for this sort of performance. Members of Congress, journalists, and minor celebrities—even Miss America—had all enjoyed the regiment's hospitality. Each guest headed home with a souvenir Ravens coffee mug and a favorable impression of the regiment's trim, crewcut commander.

From the chopper that served as his aerial command post, its seat cushions embroidered with the regimental crest and motto—Duty, with Honor—Caldwell had become adept at pointing out landmarks along his stretch of the Iron Curtain. In point of fact, visitors from the U.S. tended to find the densely wooded and minimally fortified "trace" less interesting than the quaint villages and farms of the Bavarian countryside visible below. Dressed up as educational—here is your Army defending the frontiers of freedom—the tours were actually sightseeing trips at taxpayers' expense. But the PR was good for the regiment, and it was good for its commander. Normally, it was a duty he enjoyed performing.

February in Bavaria has its own special kind of cold. The interior of a drafty Huey at 3000 feet is colder still. Today, the countryside below looked gray, forlorn, and lifeless. Any farmer with a lick of sense was home warming himself in front of his fireplace, with the family dog dozing at his feet.

In no mood for sightseeing, Big Al broke the silence.

"Bart."

The voice, though not unkind, contained hints of exasperation. Paterson had just about had it with ambitious colonels trying to make a good impression.

"Sir?"

"I'm thinking that we should scrub the visit to Rotz."

"The troops will be disappointed, sir. They've been looking forward to having you stop by."

"Perhaps, although I doubt it. Besides, I've been to border outposts, to include this one, often enough. Christ, I used to own this whole sector."

"Yessir, of course."

"Besides, our young captain down there has enough on his hands without some four-star dropping in to offer sage advice. And, yes, I know my son-in-law Lieutenant Colonel Fitzhugh Massey, III commands your 3rd Squadron and is on the ground eagerly waiting to greet us." He recited the name with something less than affection.

Caldwell hesitated to respond. The consequences of aborting the visit were difficult to calculate. But if Big Al wanted to pull the plug, Quickdraw really had no choice.

"Understood, General. Will do."

The command pilot up front had monitored the exchange on the intercom. Without being ordered, he was already wheeling back toward the regimental headquarters in Nurnberg.

Caldwell cursed silently then switched his handset to transmit.

"Raven X-ray, this is Quickdraw."

For the ops crew on duty back at regimental headquarters, instantly responding to any call from the RCO was a point of pride. Any failure on that score counted as a sign of slackness, and too many such lapses would tarnish the regiment's carefully cultivated image as a crack outfit.

"This is X-ray, Quickdraw."

A boom mic pressed against his lips, Caldwell notified the ROC that he was returning to base.

"Pass the word to Rotz. And tell Major Hicks to have our visitor's aircraft cranked and ready to return to Heidelberg as soon as we touch down."

"Wilco, Quickdraw."

In the American military tradition, reaching at least as far back as Baron von Steuben's tenure at Valley Forge, striking a balance between doing what worked and presenting a smart appearance formed a perennial imperative. Now, in the immediate aftermath of Vietnam, where nothing had seemed to work, appearances counted more than ever. The commander of the 16th ACR did not dissent from this priority. He embraced it wholeheartedly. And Paterson's decision to call off his visit to the nearby border encampment just didn't look good.

The monotonous whop-whop of the main rotor blade discouraged further conversation. Big Al himself was not known for idle chatter. Meanwhile, somewhere between mortified and enraged, Caldwell could think of nothing further to say.

That morning, confident that the Rotz visit would be successful, Caldwell had toyed with the idea of adding a personal touch to conclude the day's itinerary. Offering Massey a lift to 3rd Squadron headquarters at Pond Barracks, halfway back to Nurnberg, would allow Big Al to visit with his daughter and young granddaughters. Caldwell had felt sure the gesture would meet with warm approval. Now, it would look like a transparent effort to curry favor.

For the Lord of the Ravens, this was the last straw. The entire day had been a fiasco. One thing he knew for sure: Someone was going to pay for it.

I

Wednesday, 11 February

Albert Speer had done the Ravens no favors. In the 1930s, Hitler's favorite architect had laid out the grounds for the Nazi Party's gaudy annual rally in Nurnberg. Included in the complex was a sprawling barracks meant to house a ceremonial SS detachment.

With the coming of war in 1939, large-scale celebrations ceased. By mid-1945, the Party itself no longer existed. Soon thereafter, the SS barracks, its exterior scarred by shellfire, the huge swastika-bearing eagle ripped from its façade, became the headquarters of the 16th Armored Cavalry Regiment. Here, the regiment was to remain for decades, fixed in place by the exigencies of the Cold War.

Renamed by the U.S. Army in memory of PFC Joseph F. Merrell, an eighteen-year-old G.I. killed during the liberation of Nurnberg, Speer's formidable but graceless building had not aged well.

By the 1970s, the roof leaked, and windows needed replacing. Worse, an odor that some visitors compared to a plugged-up toilet pervaded the place. Speer's genius did not include an aptitude for plumbing.

The main entrance to Merrell Barracks, an oversized archway, opened onto a long corridor. Apart from glass cases displaying trophies won in long-forgotten sports competitions and vending machines dispensing soft drinks and candy bars, the corridor itself was almost entirely empty. A mural on the wall opposite the trophy cases retraced the regiment's heroic journey from Normandy, in late July 1944, to its arrival at Pilsen, Czechoslovakia, just prior to VE-Day. The G.I. artist, his name lost to history, had a particular affinity for burning German tanks, demolished bridges, and Old Glory waving in the breeze.

At the far end of the corridor, heavy double doors marked the entrance to the RCO's *sanctum sanctorum*. With its tall windows, twenty-foot ceilings, and parquet floor, the office itself exuded an aura suitable for the senior SS officer for whom it had been intended. To sit behind a desk that had once belonged to some Nazi *Standartenführer* had imparted to several of Bart Caldwell's predecessors a heady sense of playing a part in some vast historical drama. Direct exposure to hubris bred hubris in turn.

Leading down the hallway to the RCO's office were lesser spaces inhabited by members of the regimental staff. Lining the walls in each were plaques, certificates, and photographs testifying to past assignments at various outposts of the American imperium and to hopes—some barely flickering—for further advancement. Among officers assigned to the 16th ACR, ambition burned like a hard flame.

Major Tobias Hicks was the exception to this rule. Hicks served as regimental adjutant, a singularly unglamorous post. Adjutants do not lead charges; they push paper and douse minor bureaucratic fires. The job was one that any upwardly mobile cavalryman would avoid or escape from as soon as possible. Yet, Hicks had served as adjutant for the past year, and he appeared content to stay where he was. His very office, the walls unadorned, a single framed portrait of his wife on his desk, seemingly spoke to his professional ennui. In his case, appearances contained a modicum of truth. Here was an instance of a soldier disinclined to follow the expected path.

"Tubby" Hicks possessed many underappreciated gifts. Among them was an uncanny ability to project a sense of equanimity. As Caldwell's adjutant, he was the embodiment of serenity. Whether he had acquired this trait while riding the bench as a member of the Army basketball team or while studying literature at Oxford as the first Black West Pointer to win a Rhodes—this at a time when that university was awash with Vietnam-induced anti-Americanism—it was impossible to say. Perhaps, the quality was genetic. In any case, Tubby Hicks was seemingly unflappable. His coach at West Point thought he lacked a killer instinct, a quality that some read as akin to lethargy. Even the absurd nickname that he had acquired during plebe year—he was a well-proportioned 6'2"—left him unfazed.

Following Oxford, Tubby had completed a yearlong tour of duty in Vietnam that began with six months in the Mekong Delta advising an ARVN infantry battalion and concluded with six months as a speechwriter at MACV headquarters in Saigon. Exposing him to opposite ends of the War, the assignments imparted two mutually reinforcing conclusions. The first was that soldiers comprising the rank-and-file of the South Vietnamese army were poorly led. The second was that so, too, were the U.S. troops serving in the war zone. Both had deserved better. There was this difference, however: Whereas U.S. military leaders were alive to the crippling deficiencies in ARVN generalship, they were blind to their own comparable shortcomings.

After Vietnam, the Army assigned Tubby to teach English at West Point. While there, he reworked essays written for his Oxford M.A. into a slim but well-received study of *American "Negro" War Poetry*, an achievement that did not enhance his standing among his less intellectually inclined Army contemporaries. Poetry was for wusses, not warriors.

In truth, Tubby had never thought of himself as a warrior. That he was American, Black, and a soldier more than sufficed as sources of identity. Which component of that blend took priority was not clear even in his own mind. That the three might prove incompatible was a possibility that he was not prepared to acknowledge. On the day he swore an oath standing on Trophy Point as a brand-new plebe, he had become a novice military professional. He had spent the years since sorting out the implications of that commitment.

Among his peers, he had acquired a reputation: Here was a classic case of someone who had blown it. Now in his early thirties, Tubby was clearly failing to live up to his potential. By most conventional measures, that judgment was correct. Yet, if seemingly on the fast track to military mediocrity, Tubby appeared reconciled to that fate. Or, perhaps, he just didn't care. More often than not, his attention simply lay elsewhere.

Increasingly, it focused on the immediate past. One year after the fall of Saigon, the U.S. Army was eager to put as much distance between itself and Vietnam as possible. Most ordinary citizens concurred in this inclination. All the Bicentennial hoopla and flag-waving scheduled to culminate on July 4 had less to do with celebrating America's past than with forgetting the unpleasantness of the previous decade.

Most officers of Tubby's generation endorsed this penchant for contrived amnesia. Forgetting the entire bitter experience of the War was akin to a categorical imperative. Mulling over barely healed humiliations held minimal appeal. What purpose would it serve?

Tubby deemed his own regiment particularly susceptible to this temptation. After all, throughout the debacle of Vietnam, the 16th ACR had remained in Europe, all but unaffected by events in Southeast Asia. Across the Kingdom of the Ravens, the War's end diminished its importance even further. This fact alone provided an excuse to forgo any soul-searching.

For reasons that he himself could not quite fathom, Tubby did not share this inclination to forget. In his judgment, refusing to reckon with the War left the Ravens in a perilous position. Nothing good could come from forgetting.

Tubby's belief in the imperative of dissecting the War—scrutinizing it from every angle—had become a compulsion of sorts. His all but insatiable appetite for war-related histories, memoirs, journalism, and fiction set him apart from his fellow officers, whose literary tastes, varying according to age and seniority, ran toward *Sports Illustrated, Playboy,* and for deep thinkers, *Time.*

Although married, Tubby was a geographical bachelor, his wife Isabelle having chosen to remain Stateside, where she was finishing a medical residency at Columbia. Tubby unashamedly exploited her presence in Manhattan. Every few weeks, another request for books would arrive at Isabelle's tiny apartment. *"Dearest Izzy,"* it would read, *"I hate to be a pest, but I wonder if you could…"*

Accompanying the letter would be a handwritten list of titles, some well-known, others obscure. On weekends, Isabelle prowled among used bookstores on the upper West Side, gamely trying to fulfill her husband's request. To booksellers, she became known as the "Vietnam lady," a beautiful young Black woman with a seemingly inexplicable fetish for a particularly ugly war.

Today, as he frequently did when his boss was away, Tubby had shut the door to his office and was reading. On this occasion, however, the object of his attention was not a volume from Isabelle's most recent parcel but a brief handwritten note that had arrived with the previous day's mail.

Normally, Isabelle favored pink stationery for her personal correspondence. She had, however, on this occasion, chosen to use cream-colored card stock trimmed in blue and with Dr. Isabelle Bryce-Hicks, M.D. embossed along the top edge. Her note was dated February 2, 1976.

"Dearest Toby," it began:

> I have terrible news. We've lost the baby. It all happened suddenly, two days ago — just one of those things that wasn't meant to be.
>
> I stayed overnight in the hospital but will be back to work tomorrow. I'm feeling okay — just very sad, as I know you will be. Everyone here assures me that this should not prevent us from trying again.
>
> Call when you have a chance.
> All my love,
> Izzy

Weeks after he had returned to Nurnberg from Thanksgiving leave, Isabelle had told Tubby she was pregnant. Her reaction was one of unequivocal delight. His was more ambiguous. Although excited by the prospect of becoming a father, he worried about the implications of having a baby when Isabelle was still in training and he was serving in Europe. Now that those concerns had vanished, he felt simultaneously relieved and guilty. Above all, he felt that he had failed his wife by not being there when she needed him. His inability to speak with her directly—he had called the apartment multiple times without success—only deepened his sense of inadequacy.

An unwelcome knock on the door prompted Tubby to set Isabelle's note aside. Gracefully removing his well-shined boots from the top of his desk, he sat up.

"Come in."

It was Sergeant First Class Ezra Edwards, the duty NCO in the regimental operations center, located just down the hall. Tubby set aside the wireframed reading glasses that gave him something of a professorial look and listened carefully as Edwards passed along the RCO's instructions. When he had finished, Tubby thanked him.

"Anything else, sir?"

In his fifteen years on active duty, including one tour in Vietnam and another in Korea, Edwards had never met an officer quite like Major Hicks. He found Tubby fascinating: soft-spoken, cerebral, Black, and with a deadly jump shot anywhere inside twenty feet.

"Yes, call the airfield. Confirm that the tower knows that Quickdraw is inbound. When he's ten minutes from touching down, I want the fixed-wing that brought General Paterson here ready to return him to Heidelberg."

He waited to see if Edwards had any questions. There were none.

"As soon as that's taken care of, notify USAREUR of the change in the General's itinerary. They'll find out why soon enough. If anyone has questions, tell them to call me."

"Fully understood, sir."

"And Ezra, one more thing: Tell your guys to can the yapping about Bean Counter 6. You all must think I'm deaf."

"Roger, sir," Edwards replied, suppressing a smirk. If Major Hicks had decoded the ROC'S nickname for the regimental commander, the time had come to shelve it. On that score, a single warning would suffice.

"Thank you, Sergeant."

With that, Tubby retrieved his glasses and put his boots back atop his desk. As Edwards departed, he once more picked up Isabelle's note. He needed to ponder its implications further.

●

By the time Bart Caldwell took Big Al's hint to scrap the visit, Camp Rotz was already crawling with activity. Located just a few "clicks" from the Czech border, Rotz was one of several such small outposts for which the 16th ACR, as the forward-most stationed component of VII Corps, was responsible. Were it not for the tanks and armored personnel carriers neatly lined up inside the front gate, the site could easily be mistaken for a small minimum-security prison back Stateside, armed gate guard and rusty flagpole proudly flying the Stars-and-Stripes included.

Strands of barbed wire, strung between concrete stanchions, surrounded the entire installation, which covered a bit more than two acres. Scattered around the gravel-covered ground, patches of grass poked through the snow. Within the perimeter were a dozen poorly insulated single-story structures—frigid in the winter, stifling in the summer—that housed sleeping quarters, mess hall, aid station, supply room, offices, and a minimally equipped rec center. Elements from 3rd Squadron occupied Rotz on a rotating basis, using it as a patrol base. Currently, it happened to be L Troop's turn in the batting order.

A map spread out on the hood of his jeep, L Troop's commander—callsign Lion 6—was gearing up to exit Camp Rotz. For Captain Sydney Marks, a perpetually worried look on his dark face, reaching the accident site as quickly as possible had become priority number one. Or, at least reaching the grid coordinates that Blackbird 47, the chopper pilot who had spotted the wreckage, had reported as the patrol's estimated location.

Given the icy conditions—the roads in the Bavarian outback were hardly more than poorly marked, unpaved trails—it was going to take at least an hour to find out if that estimate was correct. By then, it would be nearly dark, with temperatures dropping. Overnight, more snow was forecast.

The word from Blackbird 47 was not encouraging. Per SOP, the L Troop patrol had consisted of two jeeps, each with a crew of two lightly armed Ravens onboard. Blackbird reported one vehicle flipped over at the bottom of a densely wooded ravine. One soldier was on the ground and did not appear to be moving. The other was nowhere to be seen. The second jeep was halted on the roadway above. Wearing army-issue parkas, mittens, and headgear with ear flaps—standard garb for February in Bavaria—the two soldiers stood alongside it, one of them shouting into a radio handset, the other furiously waving his arms in the direction of the helicopter.

This was all the information available to Sid Marks. Just reaching the site of the accident was going to be time consuming. That much was certain. Extricating soldiers, equipment, and the wrecked vehicle from treacherous terrain at night was going to be flat-out difficult.

Never during his handful of years in the Army— much of it spent on convalescent leave—had Marks dealt with a problem remotely like this. As L Troop commander, that problem was clearly his alone. Standing just yards away, his immediate boss, Lieutenant Colonel Hugh Massey, commanding 3rd Squadron, showed no inclination to come to his rescue.

Vague hopes of repairing his frosty relationship with his father-in-law had brought Massey to Rotz. With that prospect no longer on the agenda, his priority had shifted. He needed to put as much distance as possible between himself and what had the makings of a first-class cataclysm.

Bundling himself into the backseat of an OD green '72 Chevy, Massey was eager to return to his headquarters in the ancient garrison town of Amberg, a forty-five-minute drive. With her acutely sensitive antennae, his wife would already have gotten wind of the accident and would inevitably assume the worst—not for the soldiers involved but for her husband's future prospects. Connie would need settling down, before a second or third late afternoon drink prompted her to start contacting her father.

Just as he was about to exit Rotz, Massey rolled down the rear window of his sedan and motioned to Marks.

"You need to fix this, Captain," he snapped.

That was it.

Earlier in the day, with arrangements in place for what promised to be a successful VIP visit, Massey had been positively chummy, so much so that Marks had found it unnerving. As soon as radio contact with the patrol was lost and reports from Blackbird began to come in, the chumminess vanished.

As to what he was supposed to fix or how, Marks had no idea. He simply saluted and said nothing. Watching the taillights of Massey's sedan slowly disappear in the gathering dusk, Sid Marks felt very much alone.

Back in Nurnberg, his pregnant German girlfriend was waiting in the apartment that they shared. Emma understood him. No one else seemed to. So, at least, Marks had persuaded himself.

He had assumed command of L Troop barely six weeks prior. The fact that he was the only Black troop commander in the entire regiment did not boost his self-confidence. Fidgety and given to self-doubt in the best of circumstances, he yearned to fit in, not stand out. The last thing he wanted was to call attention to himself.

Now, as if to underline the solitary nature of Marks' predicament, Blackbird radioed that he was breaking station. Low on fuel and running out of daylight, he needed to return to Nurnberg.

Blackbird's departure made it apparent that nothing was going to happen unless Marks himself made it happen. A map in one hand and a radio handset in the other, Lion 6 tried desperately to formulate a plan of action. He came up emptyhanded.

His driver, PFC Hector Martinez, broke the awkward silence.

"Sir, should I get Top over here?"

"Yes, Martinez," Marks replied gratefully, "get the first sergeant."

Dismounting from the jeep, Martinez walked briskly over to a small group of L Troop NCOs who appeared to be idly shooting the breeze.

"Top, the CO needs to see you."

First Sergeant Dennis Chisholm, L Troop's senior NCO, nodded. Suppressing any inclination to hurry, he swaggered over to the troop commander's quarter-ton and leaned against the windshield. A toothpick protruded from his mouth.

"What can I do for you, Captain?"

Conveying more hesitation than authority, Marks haltingly began issuing instructions for assembling a rescue party. Chisholm interrupted him.

"Lemme handle this, Captain," he said before turning toward the nearby cluster of L Troop NCOs. "Adams, Crosby, Alexander! Drive your butts over here! I mean now!"

With Chisholm bellowing orders and obscenities, a small convoy of wheeled vehicles soon materialized at the front gate: a field ambulance, a wrecker, and a deuce-and-a-half carrying a squad of unhappy soldiers who had been looking forward to an evening in the rec center watching last year's movies on VHS.

"All set, Captain," Chisholm said. "I'll lead."

"No, I should," Marks said, mustering a show of authority.

"Suit yourself," Chisholm replied incredulously. "I'll fall in behind."

It took Marks and the hastily organized rescue party longer than expected to find the patrol. The grid coordinates provided by Blackbird had been off by several hundred meters. By the time Lion 6 reached the actual scene of the accident, it was pitch black.

His initial report, which quickly made its way through Massey to Colonel Caldwell and, eventually, all the way back to the Pentagon, was grim: Two members of L Troop, a Sergeant Peter Borski and a Specialist Danny Cotton, were dead, their vehicle totaled. The only piece of good news: The remaining members of the patrol were unharmed, if frightened. No sensitive equipment had been lost.

The men of L Troop spent the night laboring to recover the remains of the deceased and winching the wrecked jeep out of the ravine. Whether from wisdom or timidity, Marks allowed Chisholm to run things, which the first sergeant did with a great show of histrionics.

Huddled in his jeep, Marks passively watched the operation. At infrequent intervals, Chisholm swung by and went through the motions of giving a progress report.

"I've got this, Captain. Nothing for you to worry about."

Neither man showed any inclination to probe into the circumstances of the accident. What had Borski and Cotton been doing that might have caused their vehicle to slide into the ravine? The question remained unasked and unanswered.

It was approaching midnight before the entire contingent, exhausted and nearly frozen, arrived back at Camp Rotz. An ambulance was waiting to evacuate the two casualties to the graves registration detachment back in Nurnberg.

After thanking his men for their good work, Marks sent them to grab some chow and warm up. For his part, First Sergeant Chisholm showed less interest in tending to the wellbeing of the rescue party than in treating the patrol's two surviving members to a thoroughgoing ass-chewing. "Keep your mouths shut" summarized the gist of the one-way conversation.

After pouring himself a cup of mess hall coffee that was neither fresh nor hot, Sid Marks dragged himself over to the troop CP. Accidents meant investigations, more so when there were fatalities involved. Marks resolved to get his version of events down on paper while his memory was still fresh. He was determined to make his report as accurate and as comprehensive as he possibly could. He was oblivious to the fact that his own fate had already been decided.

Already, Marks had misconstrued the disaster that had befallen his command. Through no fault of his own, he had missed half the story. It would be left to others to eventually uncover the rest. In the meantime, Lion 6 had become expendable.

•

While Marks, government-issue ballpoint in hand, was organizing his thoughts, Big Al Paterson, stripped down to his skivvies, was blessedly alone in his Heidelberg BOQ suite, nursing a stiff drink. It was not his first of the evening.

Nor was it his first visit to Germany. Not by a long shot. He had fought here during World War II, with real distinction. A decade later, he had himself commanded the 16th ACR, like Barton Caldwell indulging in the delusion that it was "his" regiment. Now, he knew better. A departed unit commander was like a losing candidate for county sheriff or the emcee of a cancelled TV game show: almost instantly forgotten. As Chief of Staff, Paterson knew better than to fantasize about the Army being "his." Like every other general on active duty, regardless of how many stars they wore, he was just passing through.

In his case, passing through meant being continually on the road. Since becoming chief, he had spent half his nights away from home in one BOQ or another, and he hated them all. He especially hated the ones in Germany—the crappy, scarred furniture, the lousy mattresses, the sense that he was bunking with the malign spirit of some Wehrmacht field marshal. It had occurred to him that every BOQ on a former Wehrmacht kaserne should have a sign posted above the registration desk: "Warning—War Criminals Once Slept Here."

Travel gave him time away from Alice, always a welcome relief. But crossing all those time zones meant sleepless nights, which inevitably, in turn, led to brooding about Vietnam.

How had it happened? How had the War gone so disastrously wrong, bringing ruin to the Army to which he had devoted his life? The question nagged like a migraine headache that held his skull in a vise-like grip.

Paterson did not hold himself personally responsible for the monstrous calamity that Vietnam had wrought. God knew there was plenty of blame to go around. JFK, LBJ, McNamara, Bus Wheeler, Westy, half the press, and the whole stinking cowardly Congress: They all owned pieces of it. Even luckless Gerry Ford, who had the misfortune of occupying the Oval Office when the Republic of Vietnam had finally collapsed the year prior.

But neither could Big Al claim to be innocent. As a senior officer in the U.S. Army, Aloysius Paterson had done nothing—nothing—to impede the descent into folly, even though by 1967, at the very latest, he *knew* that the War was irretrievably lost.

Operating in the Central Highlands that year, his division chalked up a series of impressive body counts, for which he received a handsome medal and a promotion. He even made the cover of *Life* as "America's Latest Warrior-General." A gung-ho but spectacularly ill-informed journalist suggested that his achievements a decade prior, as Patton's youngest battalion commander in World War II— awarded the Distinguished Service Cross, along with several other decorations—somehow foretold a favorable outcome in Vietnam, as if the two wars were clones of each another.

If killing meant winning, then, perhaps, victory did beckon right around the corner, at least in his particular corner of South Vietnam. That was the prevailing theory, at least. But no amount of slaughter—and of U.S. troops being maimed and killed—was going to create a government in Saigon capable of actually governing or turn ARVN into an effective fighting force.

Given the right conditions, violence could create a nation. The American Revolution had shown that. It didn't take a master strategist to recognize that, in South Vietnam, the preconditions of success did not exist. In his gut, Paterson himself had known that at the time.

So did at least half the other generals on active duty. But that knowledge did nothing to impede Paterson's own willingness to order his men to launch yet another costly and futile search-and-destroy operation. Fucked-up didn't begin to describe the results.

And now, as Army Chief of Staff, he owned the consequences. The marketing theme devised for his tenure as chief was "Good and Getting Better." But, like helicopter tours and souvenir coffee mugs, this was all for show. The truth was that he presided over a broken and demoralized institution desperately trying to reinvent itself as a "volunteer force."

With plenty of fanfare but an imperfect understanding of the complexities involved, the U.S. Army had embarked upon an experiment in comprehensive social engineering. In the "old army" of Paterson's youth, white males who shared his own background and outlook had called the shots. If the "new army" was to escape the noxious legacy of Vietnam, authority would devolve to leaders who were not necessarily white or male and whose outlook differed radically from his own.

Paterson's job was to persuade the "old army" to buy into this uncertain undertaking. Although he kept his doubts to himself, on most days, this seemed like an iffy proposition, at best. With ambitious apple-polishers like Barton Caldwell waiting in the wings and conniving to take over, the officer corps sometimes appeared hellbent on repeating the errors that had led the entire Army to the brink of collapse. The very prospect was almost too much to bear.

Knowing he would regret it in the morning, he poured himself another scotch.

•

While the Army Chief of Staff was draining most of a bottle of single malt, Barton Caldwell was back in Nurnberg, having just concluded a telephone call with the commander of his 3rd Squadron. Between Colonel Caldwell and Lieutenant Colonel Hugh Massey, there was no love lost.

For over a year, Caldwell, a Citadel grad with a visceral dislike of privileged West Pointers, had proudly commanded the 16th ACR. It had recently become fashionable for senior commanders to adopt Pattonesque handles, such as *Gunfighter*, *Rampage*, or *The Dueler*. Hence, his decision to style himself *Quickdraw*. Among his contemporaries, this had become a source of quiet amusement, since Caldwell's warfighting credentials were on the thin side. Where he excelled was as a bureaucrat-in-uniform. In that sense, he was well-suited for commanding in a theater where the avoidance of actual fighting formed the ultimate definition of success. If subordinates behind his back called him *Bean Counter 6* or *BC6*, the nickname combined both ridicule and tribute. Command in U.S. Army Europe after Vietnam was a game, and Caldwell knew how to play it.

Caldwell viewed with intense suspicion Hugh Massey's direct line to General Paterson through his wife, Big Al's only child. Massey, in turn, viewed Caldwell's paper-shuffling approach to running an armored cavalry regiment with barely concealed derision. He had no doubt whatsoever that he was better suited for the job of commanding the Ravens.

He was probably right. Hugh Massey was a fourth generation West Pointer. The U.S. Army was the family firm. Both his father and grandfather had achieved general officer rank. If Hugh himself did not end up wearing at least two stars, he would retire a failure. That went without saying.

If lineage conferred aptitude, Massey seemed bound for greatness, having met with nothing but success over the course of his early career. His two tours in Vietnam culminated in command of an armored cavalry troop during the 1970 Cambodian incursion, for which he was awarded the Silver Star for gallantry. Massey had been selected for early promotion to both major and lieutenant colonel, and he was the first member of his West Point class to command at the battalion level. He was running well ahead of the pack and only too happy to let others know that he knew it. Included among these others was his boss.

Short, squat, and scruffy-looking rather than handsome—his trademark, a bushy mustache, just beginning to turn gray—Massey did not convey the classic image of a Great Captain. Neither, though, had U.S. Grant, he frequently reminded himself. And neither, for that matter, did Big Al Paterson. If being photogenic made you a winner, the widely reviled Westmoreland would have won the Vietnam War, and probably ended up in the White House.

West Point tended to instill compliance rather than foster creativity. Under the guise of educating, four years at the Academy inculcated a worldview, one that implicitly placed the U.S. Army at the center of the universe. Whatever harmed the

Army—budget cuts, for example—harmed the Republic. While there were exceptions, most graduates readily accepted this as axiomatic. As a consequence, West Pointers were more likely to excel at preserving the status quo rather than in dreaming up alternatives.

Hugh Massey was not one of those exceptions. He was a doer, or, more accurately, someone with an aptitude for making others do. Intensely focused on the matter at hand, whatever it happened to be, he was not given to introspection or to second thoughts. He would no more spend an evening contemplating "Negro" war poetry than he would hand over state secrets to the KGB.

Whatever Caldwell and Massey's personal feelings toward each other, circumstance obliged them to maintain the pretense of amiable collaboration—like Ike and Monty or, perhaps, like Fred and Ginger. This was never more the case than in disposing of that day's events.

Once Big Al had lifted off for Heidelberg from Nurnberg, Caldwell had directed the ROC to get the 3rd Squadron commander on the phone. Within minutes, Fitzhugh Massey was on the line. When the RCO picked up, he skipped past any pleasantries.

"Hugh," Caldwell said, "we need to talk about this Rotz business." He rarely called Massey by his first name. "A border incident with two troopers killed—it's a stain on the regiment's reputation."

That this stain affected his own reputation, not to mention Massey's, as well, was left unsaid.

"Yessir," Hugh answered. "If I may, I'd like to suggest a course of action."

"I'm listening."

"The issue here is one of command accountability. What happened in L Troop was unacceptable. Accountability should rest with the commander on the scene."

"So, what do you have in mind?"

"With your approval, I'll contact Captain Marks at first light and suspend him from command. He'll return to Amberg and remain here during the required accident investigation."

"Who should conduct the investigation?"

"I'd suggest that you appoint your adjutant, Major Hicks."

"Isn't he a classmate of yours?"

"Yes, but more relevant is the fact that he's Black. There are…sensitivities here that we need to respect."

"Like avoiding any impression that race plays a role in holding Marks accountable."

"Precisely. You and I fully support the Army's commitment to racial equality. That means holding everyone to the same standard. You gave Marks a shot at command. If he failed, that's on him."

In fact, Massey had opposed giving Marks L Troop, with Caldwell overriding his objections. Neither man mentioned this bit of relevant background, of which both were acutely aware.

"Okay, Hugh, I agree. We'll proceed as you suggest. But make sure you cross every T and dot every I. There can't be any suggestion of partiality here."

"Roger, sir. I fully understand."

With that, Caldwell hung up. Both he and Massey knew that an accident investigation would inevitably find something amiss: worn tires, a driver's license out of date, an incomplete pre-briefing—it didn't much matter what. The outcome would justify relieving Marks for cause, thereby allowing Caldwell to appoint a replacement. The regiment, then, could move on, with the entire episode, including the deceased soldiers, soon enough forgotten.

Neither Caldwell nor Massey took any pleasure in the scenario that was about to unfold. Neither of them had it in for the young officer chosen for sacrifice. But, for the sake of the regiment's reputation, it was essential to resolve this matter neatly and promptly.

Doing so would serve the interests of the Army as a whole. After all, scandals stemming from the conduct of the Vietnam War—most notoriously, the coverup of the My Lai Massacre—had raised doubts about the Army's adherence to the principle of command responsibility. Purging the poisons that had accrued during the War would begin with restoring that principle.

This would necessarily entail hard decisions. The career of one Prairie View A&M ROTC grad was a small price to pay to achieve that goal—and to preserve each man's own prospects for further promotion.

Thursday, 12 February

Caldwell and Massey had every reason to count on Major Tobias Hicks doing his duty, as he had twice sworn to do, first upon entering West Point and then again four years later, when he accepted his commission. They felt certain that he would not disappoint them. Tubby was a team player. So, as soon as Caldwell arrived in his office the following morning, he summoned his adjutant and gave him his marching orders.

"Find out how this happened, Major, and do it quickly. I'll expect a preliminary report on my desk by close of business. If you need help—transportation, whatever—just ask. And keep me informed. Any questions?"

It did not escape Tubby's attention that, in a regiment whose ranks included several hundred Black NCOs and enlisted soldiers, the highest-ranking Black officer—himself—had been chosen to investigate the outfit's only Black commander.

"No, sir," he replied. "No questions."

"You may not be keen to take on this assignment, Tobias. No one would blame you for that. But the regiment needs to get to the bottom of this, and quickly."

Tubby flinched ever so slightly at the RCO's use of his baptismal name. No one other than his mother and the Sisters of Mercy, who had taught him back at Holy Angels School in Chicago's Bronzeville, ever called him Tobias. Caldwell's sudden formality was both phony and presumptuous.

Suppressing the temptation to respond, Tubby saluted and turned to leave. As he stepped from the RCO's office into the hallway, he literally bumped into the Reverend Francis Xavier Scanlan, the regimental chaplain. F.X., as he was inevitably known, was a Catholic priest who had come to the Army from the Archdiocese of Chicago, a jurisdiction to which he hoped never to return.

Scanlan had nothing against Chicago—he had grown up there and still followed the Cubs. He did, however, have a problem with the local Church hierarchy, which he found suffocatingly intrusive. In his personal experience, military martinets were nothing compared to the petty tyrants who presided over the American Catholic Church.

As a recently ordained priest assigned to a prosperous Irish-American parish on the South Side, Scanlan had repeatedly banged heads with a Cardinal Archbishop convinced that he knew more about running local parishes than any pastor possibly could. Soon enough, F.X. realized that he had a choice: Either leave the priesthood, or get out of Chicagoland. It turned out to be an easy call. Today, after more than a decade in uniform, F.X. no longer thought of the Midwest as home. The Army was where he belonged and where he intended to stay.

Now a balding redhead in his mid-forties, Scanlan was beginning to put on weight. But with the armed services perpetually short of Catholic clergy, he had a keen sense of what he could get away with. That included gaining a few extra pounds and neglecting to cut his hair as prescribed by Army regulations.

As soon as Tubby saw F.X. lurking outside of the RCO's office, he grinned. His irritation at being tasked to investigate the L Troop incident eased, at least momentarily.

"Top 'o the morning to you, Padre."

"And to you, Tubby. I hear you've drawn the short straw on this unfortunate L Troop business."

"Bad news travels fast. I'll be leaving for Rotz within the hour. Probably back late tonight. Any interest in coming along?"

"Actually, I was hoping you'd ask."

Tubby had first met F.X. soon after arriving in Nurnberg. Initially bonding over their shared Chicago roots, they had since become drinking buddies and close friends.

"After yesterday," F.X. continued, "the troops down that way might be needing some good Irish sympathy. Besides, I've been stuck here at headquarters for too damn long."

"Well, I'd certainly welcome some company."

A half-hour later, a sedan was delivering the pair to the airfield where a Huey waited, its blades just beginning to turn. Whenever he left the kaserne, Father Scanlan took along the tools of his trade. He also kept a small overnight bag packed for unplanned stays. Something told him that, this time, he might be needing it. As he exited his room at the BOQ, he slung the bag over his shoulder.

While boosting F.X. aboard the aircraft, Tubby was reminded for the hundredth time how much he loathed helicopters. Something about the fumes from burning JP-4 made him feel slightly ill. He was counting on his friend's gift for nonstop banter to provide a diversion during the thirty-minute flight over to Rotz.

"Buckle up, Padre," he shouted. "With luck, we'll be back in time for dinner at Ingrid's before she closes up for the night."

F.X. grinned.

"It's your turn to buy."

●

At roughly the same time, Hugh Massey was collecting himself back at 3rd Squadron headquarters in Amberg. He had spent a long night assuring his wife that the L Troop situation was not as serious as it appeared. He and Bart Caldwell had matters well in hand.

Officers in the U.S. Army tend to be an ambitious lot. On that score, Massey set the pace among his many upwardly oriented contemporaries. Yet trailing close behind was his wife. The tragedy of Constance Massey's life was that she was born too early to receive an appointment to the Military Academy, with its traditionally all-male Corps of Cadets. She was thus unable to follow in the footsteps of her father, whom she adored.

Fitzhugh Massey was her chosen instrument for fulfilling her ambitions vicariously. Connie loved her husband enough to put up with the sex and to bear his children, but her love was inseparable from her expectations of his career success. Her personal commitment to that success was without limit. For an officer on the make, she was the perfect helpmate—or, at least, nearly perfect.

Connie had an affinity for what she referred to as "refreshments." Her preference was for vodka martinis on the rocks, either with vermouth or without. The bar in the Massey household opened promptly at 1700, sometimes a bit earlier. Connie was a high-functioning alcoholic who studiously met all of her responsibilities, even if at times, when she'd had one too many, she might become a tad imperious.

For her husband, Tubby's appointment as investigating officer figured as a plus. Massey was confident that Tubby would protect his flank. That's what classmates were for.

In fact, both knew that Tubby's relationship with Fitzhugh Massey was more complicated. True, he and Hugh had once been close friends, even rooming together during their junior year at West Point. However, the death of their third roommate,

Paul Mancino, in Vietnam, had irreparably splintered their relationship.

Mancino had not been killed in combat. He had been murdered by a Black soldier assigned to his very own unit, a victim of the Vietnam-induced toxins—drugs, racial animosity, eroding discipline—that were slowly destroying the Army.

Two days after Mancino's death, Tubby had hitched a ride on a C7 Caribou out of Tan Son Nhut to attend a memorial service for Paul in Pleiku. Hugh Massey also attended. It was the first time the two men had met in over a year. Both men mourned their roommate's passing, but Massey's grief came laced with intense, nearly uncontrollable rage.

"The bastard who did this ought to hang," he muttered when the service had ended, causing Tubby to look at his classmate incredulously.

"You mean, lynch him? Are you crazy?"

"Call it whatever you want, Tubby. He doesn't deserve to live."

"Jesus, Hugh, we don't do that." He caught himself. "At least, we don't anymore."

"Maybe, we still should," Massey said and stomped away.

At that moment, whatever affection Tubby had retained for his classmate evaporated. By 1976, their once-close friendship had long since dissolved. But they did remain classmates, a connection that, among West Pointers, took precedence over mere friendship—hence, Massey's confidence that he could count on Tubby for cover. That's what classmates were for.

As far as Massey's own role in the Marks affair was concerned, he had disposed of the hard part. Via telephone, he had just finished informing the L Troop commander of his suspension. Captain Marks was to leave Rotz and return to Amberg forthwith, bringing with him all his personal gear.

An inquiry into the events of the previous day had already commenced. Marks would learn of the results in due course.

Did Captain Marks have any questions? Apparently not—he said nothing. Without further ado, Massey terminated the conversation by hanging up.

Marks' apparent indifference struck Massey as strange. No excuses, no complaints, no begging for another chance—nothing. Here, if it were needed, was further confirmation that Marks was an odd duck. Massey had not even an inkling of how much Marks detested him.

Now, however, feeling a sense of relief that was ever so slightly tinged with remorse, Massey hollered for Greta, his German secretary, to bring him some fresh coffee. While the morning had begun on a distressing note, things were now looking up. The outlook for the rest of the day appeared promising. So, once again, did his future.

●

Back at Camp Rotz, Sid Marks was in no condition to describe what he felt. Humiliation? Betrayal? Abandonment? He had been around just long enough to know how Army investigations went: Their principal purpose was to confirm prearranged conclusions. Truth took a backseat to expediency.

He was being hung out to dry.

Marks left the L Troop orderly room for the nearby cubicle where he bunked alone—one of the ostensible privileges of command. He sat down on the iron bedstead. Minutes passed before he got to his feet and walked deliberately back to the orderly room.

"Tell the first sergeant I'm going out."

Without looking up, the company clerk nodded then returned to his typewriter.

Marks was wearing fatigues, field jacket, and a soft cap—nothing meant for cold weather. Although not visible, the side pocket of the jacket contained the .45 automatic that was his assigned personal weapon.

Immediately outside was his jeep, L-6 stenciled on the front bumper. Without summoning his driver, Marks got in, started the vehicle, and drove toward the main gate, struggling with the manual gearshift. Although surprised to see the captain driving his own vehicle, the gate guard saluted and waved him through.

Sid Marks drove several clicks away from Rotz before pulling over to the shoulder of the unpaved road. He was alone, surrounded by an impeccably groomed pine forest. He cut the engine, engaged the parking brake, dismounted, and walked a short distance into the woods, his boots leaving an imprint in the fresh snow.

In a small clearing, Lion 6 removed the pistol from his pocket and inserted a magazine. He pulled back and released the slide to chamber a round. He stood motionless, staring at the weapon in his right hand. He then released the safety, put the muzzle against his temple, and pulled the trigger. As the report echoed through the forest, Sid Marks fell to the ground, dead.

Whatever his conscious intent, his last living act was to call all kinds of attention to himself.

●

Within minutes of Sid Marks leaving Camp Rotz, First Lieutenant Jeffrey Thurlow, his XO, had a queasy feeling. Yesterday had been a very bad day for L Troop. Now, with no explanation, his immediate boss had headed off by himself to parts unknown.

A chubby blonde with a wispy mustache clinging to his upper lip, his pale blue eyes peering warily at the world through homely army-issue eyeglasses, Thurlow did not convey the image of a dashing cavalryman. Wariness translated into an aversion to exhibiting personal initiative. For many young officers, the exercise of authority did not come naturally. His commander's unexplained departure now left Thurlow unexpectedly in charge. The situation called for immediate action on his part. But action of what sort? The answer to that question was not self-evident.

That Thurlow lacked self-confidence was obvious to even the rawest recruit. A specific verbal tic reinforced his reputation for weakness. After issuing any order, no matter how trivial, he would insist that his subordinate "hop to it." Unfortunately, the tacked-on phrase came across as more of a plea than a command. To the soldiers of L Troop, he became *Lieutenant Hoppy* and, behind his back, an object of fun.

Now, after a minute's anguished hesitation, Thurlow arrived at a decision: He would allow someone else to do the deciding. From the cramped troop CP at Rotz—not much more than a radio, a phone line, and a wall map—he placed a call back in Amberg.

"I need to talk to Raven 36," he told the PFC on the other end of the line. "Right away—hop to it."

Given his less than stellar reputation, Thurlow's sense of urgency did not convey. The squadron commander was apparently in the motor pool, crawling on tanks in preparation for an upcoming regimental inspection. Massey's intense dislike of interruptions was well known. So, too, was his volcanic temper. Minutes elapsed before he finally came on the line.

"What do you want?" he demanded. "I'm busy."

Thurlow got no more than three sentences into his report before Massey erupted.

"Find him, Lieutenant," he ordered with grim urgency. "Find him *now*."

Massey slammed down the phone, and it now became his turn to collect his thoughts. This was not supposed to be happening. Now he needed to let *his* boss know that Sid Marks had literally gone off the reservation.

He immediately placed a call to Bart Caldwell, who was holding court in his office in Nurnberg, reviewing the latest statistics on the regiment's vehicle availability rate. Nervous staff officers, armed with computer printouts, stood ready to answer his questions. Why had a particular howitzer in 1st Squadron been deadlined for more than a week? Where was the engine part needed for that tank in G Troop? It was the sort of drill that Caldwell relished.

Massey insisted that the RCO come to the phone. He, too, had barely begun his report before Caldwell interrupted.

"Find him," Quickdraw 6 ordered with grim urgency. "Find him *now*."

He, too, then slammed down the phone. The monthly vehicle availability status review stood adjourned.

●

As these calls were occurring, Blackbird 41, the Huey carrying Tubby Hicks and Chaplain Scanlan, was settling onto the helipad adjacent to Camp Rotz. No one emerged from the compound to greet them.

Tubby directed the pilot to shut down the helicopter. Relieved to be back on solid ground, he dismounted and walked to the front gate, F.X. trailing behind. Inside, soldiers were hurriedly donning individual equipment and scrambling aboard every wheeled vehicle in the camp. Engines were turning over, but nothing had moved. There was furious commotion, with little purposeful action.

"Where's the fire?" he asked the obviously bewildered gate guard, who barely remembered to salute.

"I dunno, sir. Just minutes ago, everyone started running around like crazy."

"Where is your commander?"

"Well, he drove off by himself maybe a half-hour ago—maybe less. I dunno where he was going. He just left."

Tubby glanced at F.X.

"Okay, let us in, please. We'll find our way to the orderly room."

Halfway there, the pair encountered First Sergeant Dennis Chisholm. L Troop's top ranking NCO habitually affected a phony Uriah Heep-like subservience toward officers—especially those who were not white. It was an expression of contempt disguised as excessive politeness.

"First Sergeant," Tubby said, "I think you know Father Scanlan. He's checking on the troops after yesterday's incident, which the RCO wants me to investigate. But what the heck is going on here?"

"Begging your pardon, sir," Chisholm said, Tubby almost expecting him to bow and tug on his forelock. "But the troop commander drove off, and we've got orders from squadron to find him ASAP."

"What do you mean he drove off?"

"He got in his own jeep about a half-hour ago and just left. We don't know where—or why. The XO's trying to organize a search."

Chisholm's emphasis on *trying* signaled his low opinion of Thurlow.

"I'd like to see your XO."

"He's over there," Chisholm said, pointing to a line of trucks. "Lieutenant Thurlow! El-Tee!"

In short order, Thurlow was jogging toward Tubby, his unbuckled pistol belt flopping around his hips. He stopped, assumed a position of attention, and vigorously saluted.

"Okay, Lieutenant—it's Jeff, isn't it? Take a deep breath and tell me what's going on."

"Sir, the CO drove off alone. Raven 36 wants him found ASAP. I'm putting together a search party."

It was apparent that neither Thurlow nor Chisholm—nor anyone else at Rotz—knew that the 3rd Squadron commander had effectively removed Sid Marks from command.

"Okay, Jeff, this is your show, but let me make a suggestion. Before you send out your search party, let's launch the bird that brought me to look for your boss."

"Yessir, will do."

"Then, call the ROC. Are there any other Blackbirds airborne? If so, we want them diverted to help."

"Yessir."

Thurlow, however, hesitated. Lieutenants didn't usually issue orders to the ROC.

"And if anyone gives you any shit," Tubby added, "tell them you're acting on orders from Colonel Caldwell. Now, move."

Grateful for the guidance, Thurlow saluted and left on the double.

"F.X., let's you and I head over to the orderly room. German border police routinely patrol this area. They might be able to help."

At the orderly room, Tubby placed a call to the regiment's liaison with the local West German border authorities. They would keep an eye out for a missing quarter-ton and driver. As he hung up the phone, Tubby turned toward F.X.

"That's enough for now. "Let's go treat ourselves to some ghastly army-issue coffee."

"I'm thinking we're going to need it," F.X. said.

It took no more than fifteen minutes for Blackbird 41 to find the missing L Troop jeep. Only seconds later, Blackbird also located the jeep's occupant, sprawled motionless in the snow.

Out of breath and obviously distraught, Lieutenant Thurlow arrived in the mess hall with the news.

"Sir, they found the CO! It looks like he's hurt—he might even be dead!"

The XO was obviously begging for guidance. Briefly, as the full magnitude of the unfolding catastrophe sank in, Tubby reflected.

"Okay, Jeff," he said, "listen carefully. Our number one concern is to find out if your boss needs help. You've got an ambulance here and medics. I want you to personally lead the ambulance to your captain. Have Blackbird 41 talk you to his location. Understood?"

"Yessir," Thurlow replied, a bewildered look on his face.

"Get going."

Tubby turned toward the priest.

"F.X., you and I are going to commandeer a jeep with driver, courtesy of that pompous ass of a first sergeant. We need to see for ourselves what happened to Marks."

"Ah, Tubby," F.X. replied. "This is not looking good."

●

Lieutenant Thurlow arrived first at the scene, took one look at what remained of Sid Marks' face, and threw up. Apart from covering the corpse with a blanket, there was nothing the medics could do.

No more than three minutes later, Tubby and F.X. arrived, trailed by a Bundesgrenzschutz patrol in a boxy Volkswagen utility vehicle. Although Tubby had seen some badly mangled ARVN soldiers, he had never experienced anything like this. He managed to avoid emptying his stomach, but just barely.

From his own tours in Vietnam, Chaplain Scanlan had become more inured to such sights. He knelt down to unzip Marks' field jacket and briefly glanced at his dog tags.

"He's one of mine."

The priest slipped the strap of his kitbag over his head, opened it, and removed what he needed to perform Last Rites.

Not much of a believer, Tubby turned away to gather his thoughts. The day was going to be much more trying than he had expected.

Using the radio on the borrowed jeep, he contacted the L Troop CP back at Rotz. He wanted word passed immediately to Raven 36 and to Quickdraw: Lion 6 had been found and was deceased. He did not detail the circumstances. Those could wait until he could speak to each of them directly via phone. When he had finished, he turned to Thurlow.

"Look, Jeff, I know this is tough, but we've got work to do. So, listen. No one is to go anywhere near your boss or his vehicle without my personal okay. Understood?"

Without looking at Tubby, Thurlow nodded.

"And no one touches that weapon," Tubby added, gesturing toward the pistol that lay half-buried in snow. "Post guards and keep them here until I say otherwise."

Thurlow appeared to be staring at his boots.

"Jeff, look at me," Tubby said sharply. "You understand what I just said?"

Thurlow raised his eyes. His lower lip was visibly trembling.

"Yessir," he said.

"Good. You can handle this."

Tubby was not sure that he himself actually believed that. However, he had other matters to attend to, like notifying the CID. Marks' death was now a law enforcement matter.

Once F.X. had finished his ministrations, he and Tubby returned to Rotz. During the short journey, neither man spoke. Then, just as they were approaching the front gate, F.X. broke the silence.

"Did you know that Marks has a pregnant girlfriend, Tubby?"

"He does? How do you know that?"

"She's German. Daughter of a Black G.I."

"Jesus. That makes this whole mess that much worse."

Neither man said anything further until they entered the camp. With word of the suicide sweeping through the unit, Rotz itself was eerily quiet.

As soon as he arrived, Tubby went directly to the room where Marks had bunked. On the small wooden table that served as the troop commander's desk, he found what he was looking for: a handwritten, but unsigned, note. After reading it, Tubby carefully folded the note and shoved it into the pocket of his field jacket. Then, he left the room, ordering it locked until further notice.

Rotz was served by a single landline. Tubby now placed separate phone calls to Caldwell and to Massey. He provided each with a barebones account of what had occurred, but he refrained from sharing the contents of the note that Marks had written. Both senior commanders volunteered expressions of regret that sounded more cursory than heartfelt. It was apparent that neither would be shedding any tears over Sid Marks.

"I know this must be really tough on you, Hugh," Tubby said to his classmate, "losing one of your own commanders like this."

"Yes, it's certainly unfortunate," Massey replied in a flat tone. "Marks couldn't have picked a worse time to off himself, if he'd tried."

Tubby had already directed First Sergeant Chisholm to assemble every available member of L Troop in the Camp Rotz rec center. That's where he headed next. When he entered the building, they came to attention. The room was completely full.

"At ease, men."

Tubby surveyed the members of the unit as they settled into folding chairs or leaned against a wall. Before speaking, he had hoped to gauge the temper of the unit. Instead, he was met with silent resistance. As if by prior agreement, the assembled troops avoided making eye contact with him. Tubby suddenly realized that they viewed him as a stranger in their midst—an uninvited and unwelcome interloper.

With no alternative but to proceed, he broke the news.

"Men, there's no easy way to say this. Captain Marks is dead. It appears that he took his own life. We don't know why."

The room remained perfectly still. After a brief hesitation, Tubby continued.

"There will be an investigation, of course. Some of you can expect to be interviewed. Just tell the truth. In the meantime, Lion Troop's mission here continues. You all have duties to perform. The regiment expects you to perform them faithfully and diligently."

He asked for questions. There were none. Out of respect for the deceased, Tubby urged them to avoid passing along rumors and gossip—knowing that they would do so, anyway. As the men filed out, they seemed strangely unmoved. It was as if they'd never heard of Sid Marks.

By nightfall, CID had concluded its initial examination of the site, and the remains were on their way to Nurnberg. The L Troop wrecker towed the troop commander's jeep back to Rotz; now deemed cursed, no one would drive it.

It was, by now, well past dark, and the mess sergeant was eager to close down the chow line. Tubby was not particularly hungry, which made his decision to pass on chili mac with a side of greasy fries an easy one. With his pronounced aversion to skipping meals, F.X. grabbed a tray. The table reserved for officers in the far corner of the mess hall sat vacant. Tubby poured himself a cola and sat down, waiting for his friend. Neither Thurlow nor any of the other L Troop lieutenants were present. The entire dining hall was all but empty.

When F.X. had polished off the last of his fries, the pair stepped outside to grab some fresh air. It had been a very long day, and the temperature was dropping. Knowing that F.X. was a sometime smoker, Tubby asked if he could bum a cigarette. The priest reached into the pocket of his field jacket and pulled out a pack of Marlboros along with a scratched-up Zippo engraved with a map of South Vietnam. They both lit up.

Tubby spoke first.

"Shit."

"Indeed," his friend replied and paused for a moment. "How well did you know Marks?"

"Just enough to say hello to. I didn't go out of my way to befriend him."

"Majors don't usually pal around with captains."

"True, but he and I were members of the same exclusive club—Black officers assigned to the Kingdom of the Ravens."

F.X. nodded.

"A fair point," he said. "But you're not at fault."

"Maybe not, but something doesn't add up here, Padre. That's what my gut tells me, anyway. More than my gut."

He reached into his pocket and handed the note to F.X.

"I found this in Marks' room. Read it. Out loud."

"Fishhook, June 1970. I'm not the guilty one. That's all. No signature."

For a moment, there was silence.

"June 1970," Tubby eventually said, "that's Cambodia. One last futile attempt to turn the War around. But why the reference to guilt? Whose guilt?"

"Don't ask me, Tubby," F.X. said, eyeing the glowing tip of the cigarette in his hand.

"It's rough being told you're fired. I get that."

Tubby dropped his cigarette to the ground then crushed it under the heel of his boot.

"But a reason to kill yourself?" he continued. "Nah. I'm not buying it. The deaths of those two soldiers yesterday triggered something in Marks. I mean to find out what that something is."

"Tell me how I can help."

"Our esteemed regimental commander sent me here to investigate a jeep accident. That's no longer priority number one. So, I'm cutting loose Blackbird 41 and spending the night here. Starting tomorrow, I'll interview anyone in L Troop even remotely involved in the events of the past day, starting with Thurlow and that obsequious first sergeant."

"Understood."

"You can stay on with me, or head back to home station. Your call."

"You know I'll stay, Tubby."

"I figured you would."

Tubby gave his friend a playful jab to the shoulder.

"I'm grateful," he continued. "Maybe you could spend some time tomorrow just moseying around. Something's not right in this outfit. See if you can figure out what. We'll be back to Nurnberg by nightfall tomorrow. If you're up for it, I'll spring for dinner at Ingrid's."

"You're on," F.X. replied. "But in the meantime, don't even think of borrowing my toothbrush."

Friday, 13 February

Once West German police learned of an American officer committing suicide not far from the Czech border, the local press inevitably got wind of the incident. By the time Tubby and F.X. were taking their smoke break outside of the Camp Rotz mess hall, the *Süddeutsche Zeitung*, Munich's prestige broadsheet, had tapped a veteran reporter to look into the story. And that reporter was on the phone to Zaid Muhammed in Nurnberg.

Born Terrence Atkins in Valdosta, Georgia, Muhammed was an ex-GI who had stayed on in Germany after being thrown out of the Army— nominally, for illegal drug use; actually, for a pattern of disruptive political agitation. For the leadership of the 16th ACR in the late 1960s, with radicalism spreading through the ranks, this Black rabble-rouser had become a threat to good order and discipline.

To the dismay of those same American officers, Muhammed—with bad conduct discharge in hand, he had converted to Islam—subsequently managed to carve out a precarious existence as a freelance journalist, chronicling G.I.-related misbehavior across Bavaria. Brawls, sexual assaults, DWIs, traffic accidents, livestock disturbed by low flying aircraft, havoc caused by tanks rolling across cultivated fields: Whatever the incident, Zaid spun it to maximize embarrassment for the U.S. Army, with local German papers paying him a couple hundred D-marks per piece. With time, he became very adept at covering his self-assigned beat, so much so that every Army public relations officer within 100 miles of Nurnberg cordially hated his guts.

Zaid enjoyed the work, but with a wife and kids to support, he needed a regular paycheck. He was looking for the big story that would boost his chances of becoming a full-time reporter. The suicide of Captain Sydney Marks just might be that story. That Marks himself happened to be Black figured as a plus.

As he began his own inquiry, Zaid Muhammed had something that Tubby Hicks lacked: an intimate knowledge of the seedy urban landscape where mostly young U.S. troops met and mingled with mostly young working-class Germans—cheap restaurants and bars, nightclubs, and brothels. It took no time at all for Zaid to find out where Sid Marks fit in this world, including the address of the German woman he was living with. Here was the angle that would transform a humdrum suicide into a compelling human-interest story. Here, Zaid sensed, was something he could run with.

•

At Rotz the following morning, Tubby woke early and glanced at his wristwatch: Just past 0600. He had slept poorly, haunted by the image of a soldier's lifeless, mutilated body lying in blood-soaked snow. What a godawful mess. Not for the first time, he wondered what cruel irony of fate had plunked him in West Germany as the going-nowhere-in-particular adjutant of an armored cavalry regiment.

Dismissing that subversive thought, he rose quickly from his borrowed bunk, pulled on yesterday's fatigues, laced up his boots, and went down the hallway to the latrine. After splashing water on his face, he dried himself with a paper towel, trying not to think about how much he wanted to shave, take a hot shower, brush his teeth, and put on a fresh uniform. He kicked himself for not having had F.X.'s foresight in bringing along an overnight bag.

Not atypically for Bavaria at this time of year, morning fog enveloped Camp Rotz. The tops of the pines were shrouded in a blanket of gray. No Blackbirds would be flying this morning.

By the time he reached the mess hall, Tubby's mind had turned to the day ahead. F.X. was already there, nursing a second cup of coffee. Tubby walked down the chow line for the standard too-much-of-everything Army breakfast. He joined his friend, got to work on a mound of corned beef hash with eggs, and listened. The room was strangely silent. With at least three dozen soldiers at nearby tables, there was none of the usual G.I. back-and-forth. The only sound came from the clatter of silverware and plates.

"Notice anything?" Tubby asked F.X.

"Way too quiet."

Tubby nodded.

After breakfast, Tubby set up shop in Lieutenant Thurlow's office. Spare but functional, it contained a motley collection of government-issue furniture, each item more than a bit worse for wear: a gray metal desk with a vintage telephone, two steel chairs without arms, and a filing cabinet with a dented drawer that no longer fully closed. On the cement floor was a space heater of German design. Overhead hung a fluorescent light fixture. A single window, dirty and caked with frost, served chiefly to conceal the outside world. A calendar displaying the correct month and year hung on the wall. The dates prior to yesterday were crossed out. Thurlow was counting down the days until L Troop returned to Amberg.

As soon as Tubby settled himself behind Thurlow's desk, he phoned the ROC. Sergeant Edwards answered and professed great happiness at hearing his voice. Tubby responded in kind, if sardonically. He then dictated a message for Edwards to deliver to the regimental commander. It was concise and to the point: His inquiry was incomplete; he needed more time; he would provide further details by day's end.

Would the Major like to speak with Colonel Caldwell directly? He was in his office. No, Tubby replied. Inviting BC6 to meddle was the last thing he needed just now. But he reminded Edwards to make sure members of his section were tracking down next-of-kin for the three deceased members of L Troop. There was much to do on that front.

"One more thing, Ezra. I want you to run down Captain Marks' 201 file. Have it sitting on my desk when I get back this afternoon."

"Understood, Boss. Consider it done."

With that, Tubby launched into his interviews, more resigned than hopeful. He had already decided to prioritize the Marks suicide over the jeep accident, which was almost certainly attributable to driving too fast.

The Army refused to acknowledge the more fundamental cause, which was that its vehicles were inherently unsafe. Driven by soldiers barely out of their teens told to control their speed while on ostensibly vital missions, jeeps had a design defect that made them susceptible to rolling over. But rather than absorbing the cost of issuing a safe vehicle, the Army found it easier to find the driver at fault whenever a jeep flipped. That, Tubby concluded, was probably what had caused the L Troop accident. Explaining the Marks suicide was going to be more difficult.

Even so, he began by interviewing PFCs Hubbs and Wells, the two soldiers who had been trailing behind the lead vehicle at the time of the accident.

They were unhelpful to the point of being evasive. Tubby took it that they were concealing the fact that both jeeps had been driving too fast for the icy forest trails. He chose to let the matter rest there.

Next in line came Thurlow, followed by the three L Troop platoon leaders, each a second lieutenant on his first assignment. Collectively, they were a dense lot who viewed their deceased commander as something of a cypher. None had warmed to Sid Marks during his brief tenure in command. Neither had Marks gone out of his way to bond with them. Why had the jeep accident affected Lion 6 as it had? Why had he killed himself?

They each conveyed some version of utter cluelessness.

"No idea."

"Search me."

One simply shrugged.

Interviews with L Troop's NCOs proved more productive. As they crowded into the XO's office in groups of four, Tubby gradually pieced together a picture of Sid Marks as a tightly wound, nearly unapproachable loner. Back at Pond Barracks, he spent inordinate amounts of time in his office, usually with the door closed. He disseminated orders through Thurlow or First Sergeant Chisholm, with Marks himself only occasionally following up. Since Lion Troop's arrival at Rotz, he had made clear his desire to be left alone at mealtimes and after regular duty hours.

Chisholm was unsparing in his judgment.

"I don't believe the captain *wanted* to command L Troop. Once, he all but said so out loud."

"When was that?" Tubby asked.

"Just before General Paterson's visit. We was rehearsin' briefings for Big Al in the rec center, when the captain just got up and bounced his coffee cup off the wall. He said it was all a bunch of bullshit, and he was embarrassed to be a part of it. It must have been ten minutes before he calmed down. If you want my personal opinion, Major, Captain Marks wasn't cut out for command. He didn't have the right—whadaya call it—temperament."

How much of Chisholm's antipathy toward Marks stemmed from his less than enlightened views on race was difficult to say. But one thing appeared certain: As L Troop first sergeant, he had not gone out of his way to throw his struggling commander a lifeline.

Last to be interviewed was PFC Danny Martinez, who, as the troop commander's driver, had probably spent more time alone with Marks than had any other member of the unit. Martinez offered a wildly contrasting picture, depicting Marks as someone who could be warm, funny, and approachable.

"I liked him," he told Tubby.

Yet, Martinez did relate one potentially telling episode: Soon after Lion Troop had deployed to Rotz, he found Marks in his office crying, for no apparent reason. Martinez immediately made an about-face and left. Neither he nor Marks had ever mentioned the incident, although Martinez had found it very disturbing. Martinez sensed in Marks a fragility—the term he used was "jitters"—that he carefully concealed from other members of the unit.

As to the suicide, he had no better explanation than anyone else. Still, Martinez was the one member of L Troop who seemed genuinely affected by what had occurred.

•

While Tubby was interviewing members of L Troop's chain of command, Chaplain Scanlan was doing what seasoned chaplains do—making himself available to ordinary soldiers, striking up how-ya-doin' conversations, and generally checking the pulse of the unit. He casually touched base with every corner of L Troop, from orderly room and motor pool to mess hall and aid station.

He made a particular point of checking with the two survivors of the disastrous patrol. PFCs Hubbs and Wells were either still badly shaken or someone had told them to clam up. F.X. couldn't tell which. At any rate, they showed little inclination to chat and seemed eager for the regimental chaplain to move along as quickly as possible.

"Honest to God, Chaplain, if we'd seen something or knew something, we'd tell you," Hubbs said, Wells nodding in vigorous agreement. "It was just an accident. Accidents happen."

A decade of serving in troop units, on top of years ministering to clannish Irish-Americans on Chicago's Southside, had endowed F.X. with an acute ability to identify bullshit.

"You guys aren't being straight with me," he said, careful to keep a smile on his face. "But when you decide to come clean, I'll be happy to listen."

Hubbs and Wells did not return the smile. Neither did they respond.

F.X. turned and headed back toward the orderly room. His findings, it seemed, squared with Tubby's. For members of L Troop, Captain Marks had been a strangely distant figure. Except in a formal sense, he had not been a part of the unit. "I didn't really know the guy" was a common response to the chaplain's queries.

At mid-afternoon, Tubby and F.X. met to compare notes. The little so far uncovered had not brought them any closer to understanding Sid Marks.

"An enigma," Tubby said. "Do you see him differently?"

"I'm a priest, not a therapist," F.X. replied. "But if Sid Marks was a puzzling figure, we won't find the answer to that puzzle here."

Even so, they had learned whatever there was to learn at Rotz. The fog had long since cleared, and it was time to head back to Nurnberg. The Blackbird that Tubby had scheduled for 1600 hours was on the helipad and prepared to launch.

But just as the two men were exiting the front gate, a voice called out:

"Major Hicks! Sir!"

It was Lieutenant Thurlow, obviously in a tizzy, loping toward them.

"Sir, may I speak with you? It's a personal matter."

Tubby and F.X. stopped in their tracks.

"Sure, Jeff. The chaplain and I are about to leave, but we can take a few minutes. What have you got?"

F.X. continued toward the Huey until he was out of earshot.

"I need to get out," Thurlow blurted. "Out of the Army."

"Whoa, what brought this on?"

"The suicide; the accident—everything. I'm not cut out for this."

Tubby took the young officer's elbow and steered him toward a crudely designed pine bench, just beyond the helipad.

"Sit down," he said. "Help me understand what's going on here."

Thurlow was breathing heavily and did not resist, but he clearly needed time to settle down. Tubby allowed a moment to pass before saying anything further.

"Okay, Jeff, let's back up," he said quietly. "Remind me how you got your commission."

"ROTC, sir. Ball State."

"Scholarship?"

"No. I joined to please my dad. He and my mom split up when I was young, and we never got along. He used to talk a lot about serving. Being a vet is a big deal for him. I thought that, maybe if I joined up, he'd be proud of me."

"And?"

"Nothing. All he cares about is himself—and drinking."

"I'm sorry to hear that."

Again, Tubby waited.

"How much time do you owe the Army?"

"My obligation is up in June."

"But you want out, as soon as possible?"

Thurlow nodded.

"What'll you do, then?"

"I'll figure something out. I'll find a job."

"Why not stick around the Army for a while? Get the hang of things."

Thurlow had been looking down, holding his head in his hands. Now, he turned toward Tubby, his eyes wet.

"Because I'm no good at this," he said. "I'm an embarrassment. I know it. The soldiers know it. Everyone knows it."

Tubby put a hand on Thurlow's upper arm.

"Come on," he said. "You exaggerate."

"You don't know," Thurlow replied, his tone uncharacteristically testy. "You can't know. I *need* to get out."

This was no sudden impulse, Tubby realized. To deny Thurlow's request would be to subject him to needless torment. After a quick calculation, he made a decision. The Army could get along just fine minus one very junior officer.

"Okay, Jeff, we can make this happen. I want you to draft a letter of resignation. Two or three sentences, no more. Send it to me in Nurnberg. I'll get the RCO to sign off, and it will be a done deal. Your squadron commander won't interfere."

Thurlow looked Tubby in the eye and mustered the approximation of a smile.

"Thank you, sir. Thank you very much."

"No problem."

Tubby, too, smiled.

"And now," he said, "I need to get our friendly chaplain back to saving souls."

Tubby stood and held out his hand. Thurlow returned his grip for a second longer than necessary. Neglecting to salute, he then strode back toward the front gate of the encampment. Judging from his gait, he had shed a great weight.

So, perhaps the day had not been wasted, after all, Tubby thought to himself. Turning back toward the Huey, he motioned for the pilot to start the engine. F.X. was already onboard, waiting patiently while reading one of the paperback mysteries that he always carried.

As they lifted off, the smell of JP-4 turned Tubby's stomach and left him wondering whether there might not be other ways to make a living. Perhaps, Jeff Thurlow was onto something.

●

By the time Tubby and F.X. returned to the regimental headquarters, the RCO had left for the day. He and his wife had a social engagement with some local notables—not at all unusual for a Friday evening. In this case, it was dinner at the home of Nurnberg's largest BMW dealer.

The event promised to be convivial. Although Caldwell spoke only the most rudimentary German, all others present would be fluent in English. They would accommodate their American guest by speaking his language—a subtle acknowledgment of the terms of the postwar German-American relationship. Caldwell could look forward to a fine meal, with excellent wine, in a well-appointed, although unpretentious, home. The conversation promised to be pleasant and nonconfrontational. There would be no talk of politics. For at least a few hours, Bart could set aside his identity as Quickdraw 6 and simply relax. It was a welcome prospect.

Someone in the Pentagon had decided that the commander of the 16th ACR was a potential target of assassination by Red Army Faction terrorists. So, the Army had provided Caldwell with an armored sedan—a white Mercedes, no less—along with a soldier-driver trained in evasive driving tactics. The top-of-the-line car was a gratifying status symbol— elevating the Lord of the Ravens a notch above ordinary colonels who trundled around in glamor-deprived Chevies and Fords.

With reason, therefore, he welcomed the prospect of a half-hour drive from his quarters to the upscale neighborhood where their hosts lived. Settling back in the comfortable leather backseat, he half-listened to Harriet as she gossiped about the latest controversies among members of the regimental officers' wives club.

"Harriet, if I did half as good a job running this regiment as you do running the Nurnberg OWC, the Soviets would give up, and we'd win the Cold War."

"Oh, hush. You don't know half of what we've got going on. And that's probably just as well. Gives you less to worry about."

Caldwell could not have asked for a better life partner: His wife was hard-working, loyal, and equally adept at running a household or entertaining. Always well-groomed and well-dressed, she carried herself like the wife of a senior officer. She also possessed a pronounced sense of propriety. A Southerner like her husband, Harriet had been raised to believe in tradition. Things needed to be done right. When they weren't, she spoke up, as she was doing now, in recounting social infractions committed by a rambunctious group of young 1st Squadron wives.

As Harriet shared this source of her distress, Caldwell's mind wandered to the matter of the L Troop commander's suicide—not as a personal tragedy, but as an unforeseen disruption with the potential to produce all sorts of unwelcome complications.

Bart Caldwell liked to think of himself as a broad-gauged, forward-looking military officer surrounded by stodgy contemporaries. He had, in fact, developed heterodox, if not downright heretical, views regarding what role the U.S. military was actually playing in the ongoing Cold War. Sharing those views would not work to his advantage career-wise—to put it mildly—so he kept them to himself.

The official and widely accepted line out of the Pentagon was that U.S. forces in Europe—indeed, the entire U.S. Army, now that the unfortunate distraction of Vietnam had ended—existed to deter Soviet aggression and thereby prevent World War III. Uncritically endorsed by the press and both political parties, this line of argument imparted to U.S. policy abroad and to U.S. politics at home a reassuring continuity.

Bart Caldwell found great comfort in continuity. He loathed surprise or disruption. After all, the status quo existed for a reason. Except in the rarest of circumstances, its preservation worked to the benefit of all—or, at least, of most.

So, while he would cast an absentee ballot in the coming November election—doing so, after all, was a civic duty—he would vote knowing that it didn't particularly matter which candidate or which party came out on top. Whatever the outcome, certain things were assured, not least among them that the very formidable 16th ACR, with its several thousand soldiers, would remain in place along the Czech border as part of a very large U.S. military force permanently stationed to Western Europe.

After considerable reflection, Caldwell had concluded that this U.S. presence in Europe had almost nothing to do with preventing World War III. After all, if the Soviets had any interest in overrunning Europe, wouldn't they have taken the opportunity to do so when a half-million U.S. troops were bogged down in Southeast Asia? What better moment to make their move?

Far from plotting to expand their empire, the Soviets already had their hands full just hanging on to the empire they had. If ordered by the Kremlin to do so, Russian conscripts would no doubt attack into the heart of NATO. But would conscripts from East Germany, Czechoslovakia, Poland, Hungary, and other satellites willingly join in? Given the uprisings that had roiled the Eastern Bloc in the 1950s and 1960s, that seemed unlikely, at best. Indeed, under such duress, the Warsaw Pact might simply unravel, with incalculable risks to the Soviet Union itself.

In other words, the canonical Cold War scenario—a massive Communist assault out of the East—did not stand up to close scrutiny. This did not, however, rob that scenario of utility. Caldwell had come to appreciate the way that expectations of a Warsaw Pact attack—however fanciful— sustained a vast network of power and privilege that, among myriad other things, found him being driven to dinner at government expense in a large Mercedes Benz with glove-soft leather interior.

Caldwell was both personally and professionally invested in sustaining such arrangements. Indeed, his ultimate ambition in life was to achieve four-star rank as commanding general of USAREUR, with an even bigger car and spacious villa-like quarters on a hill overlooking Heidelberg.

The never-ending round of maneuvers, weapons qualifications, and war-planning exercises, not to mention surveillance patrols along the Iron Curtain, would continue more or less in perpetuity. It wasn't real soldiering, of course. It was actually something much better. It was playacting, dressed up with all manner of lethal props, from small arms to tanks and artillery. And he would be damned if he was going to let some suicidal Black captain screw it all up…

"Bart, darling!"

Harriet's voice jerked him out of his reverie.

"We're here."

They had arrived at their host's home. Herr Somebody-or-Other was waiting at the front door to greet them.

Caldwell shook himself fully awake, exited the car, and took his wife's arm. The Lord of the Ravens had arrived.

●

The RCO's absence for the evening was fine with Tubby, who scratched out a brief report, which he placed in the middle of Quickdraw's desk. He had learned nothing at Rotz that couldn't wait until Monday morning, when he promised to provide a complete update. If Caldwell needed something sooner, the ROC knew where to find him.

Tubby picked up Marks' 201 file, which, as promised, was on his desk. Even for a young officer, it was surprisingly thin. To read it undisturbed, Tubby decided to take it back to his BOQ. Then, after assuring himself that efforts were underway Stateside to notify the next of kin of the three deceased Ravens, he once again called Isabelle's apartment. It was now midday in Manhattan, and she was almost certainly at work. Still, it was worth a shot. After allowing the phone to ring a dozen times, he gave up.

Muttering a string of expletives, Tubby closed the door to his office, told the ROC where he would be that evening, and walked across the parade ground to his BOQ, at the opposite end of the kaserne.

Tubby's quarters—a bedroom with a shared bath—had not been chic even when built in the mid-1930s, during Nurnberg's heyday as the spiritual home of the Nazi Party. The furniture was army-issue, except for a dark green upholstered chair with accompanying reading lamp, both purchased at his personal expense. The room also contained a waist-high bookcase stuffed with books, most Vietnam-related. Atop the bookcase was a three-year-old photo of Isabelle, along with back issues of the *New York Review of Books* and the *New Republic*. A high-end Sony turntable, purchased at the PX, had a McCoy Tyner LP cued up and ready to play. He carefully placed the needle on the record and adjusted the volume.

It took Tubby no more than 15 minutes to shave, shower, and brush his teeth—one of the few useful things he had learned at West Point was how to address such personal needs without undue delay. Donning jeans, a navy-blue turtleneck, black ankle boots, and a dark brown leather jacket with scarf, he was about to head out when someone rapped on the door.

"Come in. It's unlocked."

It was F.X., decked out like the Hollywood image of a Catholic priest: black wool overcoat, black fedora, black shoes, black everything.

"Wow—hot date tonight?"

"Stuff it, Major, let's go eat. And what's that noise?"

He gestured toward the turntable.

"It's called jazz."

"I don't get it," F.X. replied. "Never have."

"That's okay. I don't *get* Gregorian chant."

As F.X. laughed, Tubby grabbed his keys, and they were out the door. The night was crisp but clear, with a half-moon—perfect conditions for walking the several blocks to the Goldener Fuss, the neighborhood gasthaus that had become their favorite hangout.

Ingrid and Hans Becker had opened their restaurant in the late 1940s, just as Nurnberg, shattered by Allied bombers, was being rebuilt. They had run it ever since. The place oozed Gemütlichkeit, the coziness that Germans—Bavarians, above all—cherished. The furnishings were dark and dated, the walls covered with soccer memorabilia. In one corner was a floor-to-ceiling porcelain stove, which had, somehow, managed to survive the war. It threw off enough heat to warm an amphitheater.

Stout and in her sixties, Ingrid waited tables and kept watch over the rest of the small staff. The rarely seen Hans handled the kitchen. He had learned to cook in the army. Like most West German veterans of World War II, he insisted that he had served exclusively on the Eastern Front, thereby dodging awkward questions about whether he had killed any Americans. Tubby and F.X. were fond of them both.

Once they had settled at a corner table, Ingrid approached with a beer in each hand.

"The usual, I presume, gentlemen?"

"Danke," F.X. replied, reaching for his glass even before Ingrid had set it down. He took a large swallow, wiping the foam from his mouth with the back of his hand.

"Ah!" he said, with undisguised delight.

"Not very dignified for a man of the cloth," Tubby teased.

"Just drink up."

With other customers in need of tending, Ingrid interrupted the repartee.

"And what will you gentlemen be having for dinner tonight?"

She had not brought a menu, knowing that Tubby and F.X. had each long since committed it to memory.

"Zigeunerschnitzel mit pommes, bitte," F.X. said, without hesitation.

"A lot of calories there, Padre," Tubby said with a pretense of concern.

"Well, it's been a long day, and I'm hungry," F.X. replied with a pretense of annoyance.

"And you, Major?" Ingrid asked.

"A bowl of Hans' fabulous Kartoffelsuppe, bitte. Mit brot."

"A prudent choice. Coming right up."

As Ingrid walked away, a slender Black man of about thirty, with a formidable Afro, approached their table. His look was late-Sixties urban casual: faded jeans, wide leather belt, dark tee shirt, and a U.S. Army field jacket, frayed around the cuffs and displaying no rank. Tubby had no trouble recognizing Zaid Muhammed.

"Greetings, Chaplain. Good evening, Major."

"What can we do for you, Herr Muhammed?" Tubby asked in an even tone.

Zaid tried his best to conjure up an ingratiating smile.

"I've come," he said, "to lend you my expert assistance."

"Really?" Tubby asked. "How so?"

To conceal his irritation at having their evening disrupted, F.X. stared moodily into his beer.

"I'm here to offer you a deal."

Without being invited, Zaid grabbed a chair, spun it around, and sat.

"Major," he continued, "I've heard you're investigating the untimely death of Captain Sydney Marks. Well, I've got a promising lead on why he killed himself. You don't, and I'm willing to help you solve the mystery."

When Tubby did not respond, Zaid went further.

"Does the name Emma Maier mean anything to you?" he asked.

"Not one I'm familiar with," Tubby answered.

"She's Sid Marks' girlfriend. Her father was a Black G.I., now long gone. Emma is also the mother of Sid's unborn child."

"So?"

"So, I've met her—pretty sad kid, not that your Army gives a damn. She says she knows why Marks killed himself. I'd say she's worth listening to."

"What's in it for you?

"Well, as a journalist, I'm always interested in truth seeing the light of day," he said sarcastically. "But there's more in this case."

"Like what?" Tubby asked.

Ingrid set two small salads down on the table, briefly interrupting the exchange.

"Marks was badly wounded in Vietnam, and not just his body. He witnessed something—I'm pretty sure it was in Cambodia—that messed him up."

"Vietnam messed up everyone who served there," Tubby countered.

"Some more than others," Zaid shot back. "Marks was wounded in more ways than one. But here's the point: Emma Meier knows things. What she knows implicates senior officers in big-time wrongdoing. Maybe not Watergate, but bad enough—possibly war crimes. It's those big fish I'm after."

"So, what do you want with me?"

"I think you should go see Emma Meier. I guarantee you'll find it worth your while."

Zaid looked Tubby squarely in the eye.

"You're supposedly a straight-shooter, Major, someone who does the right thing because it's right. If it'll help, I'll even take you to her apartment."

With that, the journalist abruptly rose from his chair, put a slip of paper containing his name and phone number on the table, and walked out.

As if on cue, Ingrid arrived with the meals. Suspending the requisite grace, F.X. grabbed his fork and knife, then attacked dinner. Tubby watched, both amused and amazed.

"Well, my hungry friend," he said, "what do you make of all this?"

F.X. hesitated, carefully chewing on a piece of schnitzel.

"I think you should go see Emma Meier, and the sooner the better."

"I suppose so," Tubby replied without enthusiasm. "Tell you what: I'll call our enterprising cub reporter when we get back to the Q."

With that, he pocketed Zaid's slip of paper and turned his attention to his soup. It proved to be as good as always.

"Let's have another beer."

Saturday, 14 February

U nless duty interfered, Tubby reserved his Saturday mornings for pickup basketball with the troops. This particular Saturday was Valentine's Day, and Tubby congratulated himself for having remembered to send Isabelle a small gift. He only hoped that it had arrived on time.

After brewing a cup of instant coffee and helping himself to a yogurt from the small frig in his room, he changed into shorts, tee-shirt, and a faded gray sweatshirt with ARMY across the front. Lastly, he laced up a pair of sweat-stained Converse All-Stars.

By the time he had jogged over to the austere post gymnasium—another dingy artifact of National Socialism—some two dozen young soldiers were on the court loosening up and practicing jump shots around the arc. They had been waiting for "the Major," the catalyst for what had become an unofficial highlight on the weekly calendar of events at regimental headquarters.

When the new day eventually dawned back Stateside and the sun traversed the Continent from east to west, young men would enact a similar ritual in countless gyms and, weather permitting, in as many schoolyards: full-court, five-on-five, shirts-and-skins, call your own fouls, one point per basket, first team to fifteen wins—and the winner keeps the court.

The pool of Raven ballplayers this day consisted of a few high school hotshots, a larger number of youngsters who had learned the game on public courts in the rougher parts of big cities, and one lieutenant who had played ball at a small Baptist college in Arkansas. Roughly half were Black and half not.

Tubby picked four for his squad, seemingly at random but ensuring a semblance of racial balance. The rest organized themselves into several teams and flipped coins to decide who would get the first crack at Tubby.

Built like a small forward, he preferred to play point guard. Nobody was going to question the Major's prerogative to do so. Tubby's style of play emphasized discipline and teamwork. Handling the ball, finding the open man, setting the pick, starting the fast break, hustling back on defense: For Tubby, these defined the essence of the game. Although he rarely shot, his team almost always won—much to the dismay of the run-and-gun hotdogs who deemed basketball an individual sport.

Up and down the court, they ran, game after game. The score meant nothing—and everything. Finally, dripping with sweat and nearing exhaustion, Tubby announced that he was calling it quits. As usual, his team was undefeated.

"That's enough for me, guys. You've about run this old-timer into the ground."

They crowded around him to shake hands.

"Thank you, sir!"

"Good game, Major!"

"See you next week?"

Tubby pulled on his sweatshirt and went outside. The cold air was bracing. An imbiss adjacent to the gym—basically, a small trailer—sold the German equivalent of street food to soldiers and civilian employees. After asking for a bottle of mineral water and a currywurst, he gave the Turkish proprietor a handful of D-marks.

He immediately drained the bottle then took a moment to catch his breath, the adrenaline slowly draining away. He felt glorious. Tubby eagerly looked forward to the day when he and Isabelle would reunite. And he entertained hopes of one day having a family. But when it came to pure unadulterated joy, nothing came close to what he was feeling at that very moment.

The wurst was ready, slathered in sauce and nestled in its white cardboard sleeve. Using a small disposable wooden fork, Tubby lifted it from the counter, took a bite, sighed, and sauntered back toward the BOQ. If only every day in the Army could begin as this one had.

•

Back in his room, with McCoy Tyner on the turntable, Tubby took a few minutes to cool down. A paperback copy of *The Quiet American,* Graham Greene's unsettling account of lust, ambition, and illusion in French Indochina, sat on the table alongside his reading chair. He flipped it open and found himself reflecting yet again on its themes of cynicism, calculation, and betrayal.

This was not Tubby's first encounter with the novel. He found the story of Thomas Fowler, the beautiful Phoung, and Alden Pyle irresistible, and he sensed that, with each reading, he came incrementally closer to unearthing some deep truth about the War and his own country. A full decade before U.S. combat troops began arriving in-country, Greene had anticipated with prophetic accuracy what America's fateful encounter with Vietnam would yield.

Had Pyle's relationship with Fowler ever allowed room for anything genuine? Or, had it, from the outset, been based on deception and mutual contempt? And how had Greene himself foreseen with such precision the blunders that the United States was destined to perpetrate in Vietnam? Was it his visceral disdain for all things American that enabled him to see things to which others were blind? Tubby found the mere thought deeply disconcerting.

But today, that thought would have to wait.

He had agreed to meet Zaid Muhammed at 1230. After showering and donning a fresh set of civvies—

aquamarine Nikes, this time, instead of boots—Tubby left the BOQ and walked toward the front gate of the kaserne. Zaid was already waiting when he arrived.

"Right on time, Major."

"Thank you. What now?"

"We catch a bus—more than one, actually. Emma lives out near Furth."

They walked a half-block to the nearest bus stop and waited. They made a striking pair, two Black Americans, one tall, good-looking, and impeccably turned out, the other short, frowzy, and badly in need of a shave. Apart from Zaid telling Tubby which bus to board, where to get off, and how to transfer, neither spoke. Then, Zaid broke the silence.

"Tell me, Major, has anyone ever called you 'nigger'?"

"What kind of stupid question is that?"

"I don't mean to be insulting. But you're a Black guy, and yet, somehow, you seem so—what's the word? Mellow? Serene? I mean, are you really Black?"

"Yes, I am really Black."

Tubby bit off the words.

"But has anyone ever called you 'nigger'?"

"To my face? Not lately. Back in Chicago, when I was a kid? Yes, of course. What's your point?"

Tubby very rarely lost his temper. This was threatening to become one of those rare occasions.

"No real point," Zaid said. "I'm just trying to figure out which team you're on."

Tubby vaguely recognized the legitimacy of the question, although it was not one that he was inclined to contemplate.

"Who says I have to choose?" he asked. "I'm a Black American who also happens to be a soldier."

"And a Raven," Zaid said, sticking the needle in deeper.

Tubby grabbed the bar of the seat in front of him and gripped it between both hands.

"Yes," he said, "also a Raven, I suppose."

"No contradiction in any of that?"

"None that can't be surmounted."

Zaid's interrogation was testing the limits of Tubby's patience. It was time to turn the tables.

"But let me ask you," he said, "whose side are *you* on?"

"I stand with my Black brothers."

"Like Captain Marks, I suppose."

"Like Captain Marks."

Zaid paused.

"As you should," he added.

"When I need your advice, I'll ask for it," Tubby replied curtly.

Both men fell silent for the remainder of the trip. When Zaid announced their arrival, they dismounted the bus. On the sidewalk, neatly made of paving stones, Tubby paused to get his bearings.

It was a neighborhood of long three-story apartment buildings, constructed of cinder block, with an overcoat of stucco, and painted in peeling pastels. Hastily thrown together soon after World War II, they now housed those who inhabited the bottom rungs of the working class, mostly Turks invited into Germany to make up for a postwar labor shortage. That Emma Maier lived in this neighborhood signaled that West Germany's highly touted "economic miracle" had left her behind.

Zaid led Tubby to Emma's flat, located in the basement of the nearest building. Knowing that they were expected, he knocked and entered without waiting for a response.

"Emma? Zaid here. I've brought along Major Hicks."

The front door of the apartment opened directly to a living area that was small, dimly lit, and crammed with cheap furniture. At the far end was a television, broadcasting reruns of an American sitcom—free entertainment, courtesy of the Armed Forces Network. Atop the TV were framed photos of Emma with Sid Marks, reminders of better days. In one, they were wearing stylish ski gear and looking very happy.

In the center of the room stood Emma herself, now anything but happy and looking very pregnant in a nubby gray bathrobe. With the possible exception of Sid Marks himself, no one would accuse Emma Maier of being beautiful. With an olive complexion and stringy blonde hair, she was very plain—just this side of homely.

She peered at Zaid and Tubby as if they were apparitions.

"May we come in?" Zaid asked, belatedly.

"Yes, of course."

A tissue balled up in one hand, Emma had obviously been crying.

"Please, sit down," she added. She spoke English haltingly and with an accent.

Emma sat down heavily in a kitchen chair while Tubby and Zaid settled onto a sagging brown sofa.

"Fraulein Maier," Tubby said, "allow me to introduce myself. I'm Major Hicks. You already know Herr Muhammed. I serve in the regiment where Captain Sydney Marks was assigned."

Emma dabbed her eyes. Whether she was actually listening was unclear. Even so, Tubby pressed on.

"We all feel terrible about what has happened. My boss, Colonel Barton Caldwell, has asked me to find out what might have led Captain Marks—Sid— to take his own life. I'm hoping that you might know something that can help us."

Tubby stopped speaking. An awkward silence descended on the room, which Emma herself finally broke.

"Why should I help you? Who is helping me?"

As she spoke, she gestured toward her unborn child.

"Even my own mother blames me for making the same mistake she did."

At a loss for how to respond, Tubby lunged for the nearest cliché within easy reach.

"I'm very sorry."

Emma pretended not to hear him.

"Sydney told me about you," she said. "He called you a house nigger."

Tubby flinched but said nothing. At the far side of the room, the laugh track from *The Brady Bunch* rose then receded with rhythmic regularity. Zaid reached over and turned down the volume.

"Emma," he said, "Major Hicks means well. He wants to help. So do I."

"You want to know why my Sydney killed himself?" she asked, her voice becoming shrill. "I don't know why. What I do know is that it is your fault—your Army's fault."

For a moment, she fell silent.

"Or, perhaps, it was the War. You know that Sydney was badly hurt in Vietnam."

"I know he was wounded," Tubby said, Emma looking at him with contempt.

"You don't know how badly," she replied. "Only I know that."

Again, she hesitated, as if exhausted by the effort to recall painful events.

"We met more than a year ago, when he first joined your unit. *Ravens*, you call yourselves? What a silly name. I was lonely, and he was nice. We fell in love, and I invited him to move in. Then, things started to change. Sydney has—had—difficulty sleeping. He had terrible nightmares. And I will admit that he drank too much. Much too much. And when he drank, he would get very cross."

"Did he hurt you?"

Zaid was now asking the questions.

"No, he never struck me. My mother says that my father would hit her. Sydney never once hit me. He was a good man. He would have been a good father. Now, I don't know what will happen to me. Or to this baby."

"What was he cross about? Did he describe the nightmares?"

"It was always about the War. Sydney was there when you Americans invaded Cambodia. He saw things that upset him—things he could never forget."

"What sort of things?"

"I don't know exactly. But they involved killing—killing women and children."

"Did he participate in the killing?"

"No. At least, I don't think so. But he saw things. He never talked about the details. But the officer in command was one of you Ravens. Sydney told me."

"That officer's name?"

"I don't know it."

"Did Sydney talk about this with anyone else?"

"I'm not sure. Sydney was seeing a priest. He might have told him things."

"What priest?"

"You should know. He is from the Army. I never met him. Father Scanlan, I think his name is."

Tubby sat motionless, struck dumb. Zaid struggled to keep a straight face.

After another few moments, Tubby stood, signaling his intention to depart. They would leave Emma to grieve alone. As soon as they left the flat and the door was closed behind them, Tubby turned on Zaid.

"You knew that Chaplain Scanlan had been seeing Marks," he said sharply. "Why didn't you tell me?"

"Easy, Major, I don't work for you. And I didn't actually *know*. I just suspected, okay? Besides, the real question is why your bosom buddy Scanlan didn't let you in on his secret. Any ideas?"

Tubby did not respond. That was, indeed, the question, which he mulled over as they made their way back toward the kaserne without further conversation. Obviously, he and F.X. needed to talk.

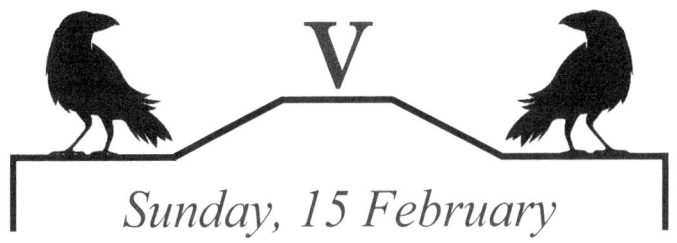

V

Sunday, 15 February

For the regimental chaplain, Sunday was never a day of rest. Mornings began with multiple masses in the small unadorned Merrell Barracks chapel that he shared with his Protestant counterpart—when it came to religion, the Army was a model of ecumenism. Following each mass came coffee and donuts in the church basement, or some more elaborate celebration of Baptism, First Communion, or Confirmation. Doing the Lord's work would occupy F.X. for most of the day.

Larry Kaplan, veteran *New York Times* foreign correspondent, did not take it upon himself to do the Lord's work. As a result, he could usually count on taking Sunday off. But today was not one of those days.

In Innsbruck, the 1976 Winter Games were just wrapping up. After watching the Soviets defeat Czechoslovakia to earn their fifth hockey gold medal—the *Times* headline: "Soviet Wins in Hockey; U.S. Fails"—Kaplan was headed by train to Munich then onward to his apartment in Frankfurt. Back in New York, however, the foreign desk wanted him to divert to Nurnberg. The suicide of U.S. Army Captain Sydney Marks a short distance from the Czech border was attracting attention in the German press. Was there a story here? New York wanted Kaplan to find out. To kick off his inquiry, Kaplan's editor had given him the phone number of a Nurnberg-based freelancer of dubious credentials. His name was Zaid Muhammed.

Arriving at the Nurnberg hauptbahnhof in late afternoon, Kaplan checked into Le Méridien Grand, a very old hotel restored to its prewar opulence. If the home office was going to keep him from spending the night in his own bed, he figured it could spring for pricy digs.

After settling into his nicely appointed room, Kaplan phoned Zaid, who was both surprised and pleased to receive a call from someone employed by such an august American newspaper. They agreed to meet for breakfast the next morning. Kaplan also placed a call to the headquarters of the 16th ACR. Although no one in a position of authority was available on a Sunday, he left his name and asked for a call back. He then went downstairs to treat himself to dinner and drinks, courtesy of his employer.

Kaplan himself was an ex-GI—drafted in 1942, midway through his sophomore year at Penn. Trained as a rifleman with the Army's 28th Infantry Division, he came ashore at Normandy seven weeks after D-Day and served with his unit until the war ended. By then, he had matured into a seasoned, competent, and very lucky squad leader.

In October 1945, he mustered out as a staff sergeant with no particular plans. Rather than making a conscious decision to pursue journalism, he drifted into it, thereby discovering his calling. The early Sixties found him in Vietnam, reporting alongside such luminaries as Neil Sheehan, David Halberstam, and Malcolm Browne. Like them, he was an early supporter of the War who came to see it as a colossal mistake. But Kaplan was not one to relitigate the past. Vietnam was over. Restoring the U.S. military to health, he believed, should now figure as a national priority.

By the mid-1970s, for many younger American journalists, anti-military posturing had become a badge of honor, akin to despising Richard Nixon and J. Edgar Hoover. Kaplan remained stubbornly unfashionable. No longer the spry young infantryman—he was balding, pudgy, and taking meds for hypertension—he sympathized with those willing to serve at a time when military service was anything but popular. The suicide of a young Black captain who was a Vietnam vet was not an obvious story for the *Times* to cover. In fact, it might not be a story at all. Still, it was worth exploring.

●

Tubby was not a churchgoer, so his Sunday routine did not include religious services. It did, however, involve a ritual of sorts: writing letters home.

After rereading Isabelle's latest missive, he would carefully reply, using a fountain pen that she had given him when he won the Rhodes. This was a task that he found immensely gratifying, even though it typically consumed most of the morning. Some people communed with God; apart from the occasional and very brief trans-Atlantic phone call, this was Tubby's way of communing with his wife. He viewed it as a sacred obligation.

This morning's letter was not going to be an easy one to write. Much to his dismay, he had still not been able to speak with Isabelle since her miscarriage. Now, at a very minimum, he owed it to her to describe his feelings, which were conflicted. And he also needed to respond to the longer letter she had written just a day prior to losing the baby. It had contained welcome news, but here, too, his feelings were complicated.

Nearing the end of her residency, Isabelle had begun to receive job offers. Her timing could hardly have been better. Whether for principled reasons or for show, large American institutions— corporations, universities, hospitals, government agencies—were now competing to hire talented and accomplished women. Izzy was both. Invitations for her to join top medical centers had begun to materialize. She found two especially tantalizing: the University of Chicago Medical Center, located in their hometown, and UCLA, on the West Coast. Neither was located in proximity to a major Army post.

The incompatibility of Isabelle's career trajectory with any aspirations that Tubby might have for staying in the Army was becoming difficult to ignore. In describing the opportunities on offer, she was conveying the gentlest sort of ultimatum.

Tubby's reply dodged the elephant in the room. Instead, after expressing his sorrow about the baby—"we will get through this"—he pivoted to a less emotionally fraught topic, providing his wife with a detailed account of the Sydney Marks affair. He concluded by mentioning his frustration with F.X. for concealing his connection with Marks. Of course, for the moment, Tubby was concealing from Isabelle his own growing uncertainty about his future in the military. He did not want to raise any false hopes.

After writing shorter notes to his mother, still in Chicago, and to his sister, who lived with her family in Winnetka, Tubby posted the letters. Then, as was his Sunday custom, he set out to explore the city that was his temporary home.

The day was cold but clear, ideal for walking. On Sundays, traffic was light, and with most stores closed, few pedestrians were about. With a typically colorful and intricately folded German map in hand, Tubby headed toward the Pegnitz River, which bisected Nurnberg's city center.

Barely thirty years before, in the course of a single night, a massive raid by RAF Bomber Command had turned the Altstadt into rubble. A comprehensive postwar restoration project, now nearing completion, had faithfully reconstructed hundreds of buildings, many of them centuries old. Also salvaged were the many small bridges spanning the Pegnitz. Tubby found these especially charming. Intimately familiar with the results of "urban renewal" in the Chicago neighborhood of his boyhood, he saw in this German commitment to architectural preservation a rebuke of American civilization. Barbarism can take many forms.

Refreshed upon returning to his BOQ hours later, Tubby spent the balance of the afternoon listening to music while sifting through the contents of Sid Marks' 201 file. It presented a perplexing picture. Nearly six years had elapsed since his evacuation from Cambodia. Marks had spent most of that time under a doctor's care, either in hospital or on an outpatient basis while on convalescent leave. His physical wounds, while serious, did not adequately explain his long absence from full-duty status. Although now wearing captain's bars, in terms of actual experience, he was still a raw lieutenant. Put simply, he had not paid his dues. Nothing in his record suggested that he was ready to command an armored cavalry troop on the Czech border. Tubby was left wondering why the Army had even retained him on active duty.

Yet the 201 file had revealed one very startling fact. During his very abbreviated combat tour, Marks had served with A Troop, 1st Squadron of the 17th Armored Cavalry Regiment. Tubby was almost certain that Hugh Massey was commanding B Troop when the 17th ACR entered Cambodia.

On Sundays, the *Goldener Fuss* was closed, so as dusk approached, Tubby reluctantly decided to have dinner at the small Merrell Barracks officers' club. This was not an appealing prospect. Everything about the O-club was dated, to include the menu. But with the approach of a new work-week dampening his spirits, he needed some cheering up. At the club, there was at least some chance of running into a friendly face.

As he left his room, he stuck a note under F.X.'s door, telling the priest where he would be. Then he stopped by the ROC, crowded with radios, telephones, and clipboards displaying various status reports. Covering one wall was a map of the entire regimental sector, with symbols showing who was doing what throughout the Kingdom of the Ravens. The ROC stood at the center of its own self-contained solar system. Tubby found the constant din of submitted-and-acknowledged reports strangely comforting. Here was order and routine, and a semblance of purposefulness.

The duty NCO informed Tubby that Quickdraw 6 was flying to Camp Rotz late the following morning. While there, he would preside over a memorial service for the three deceased members of L Troop. The regimental chaplain would surely attend, as would the 3rd Squadron Commander. Tubby asked if there might be any spare seats on the RCO's bird, knowing that there would be. Attending the service would allow him to update both the RCO and Hugh Massey on his preliminary findings.

From the ROC, Tubby headed toward the club, cutting diagonally across the gravel-covered parade ground. A bugle interrupted his passage. From roof-mounted loudspeakers, a tinny recorded version of "Retreat" began to play. Every Raven within hearing distance, Tubby included, assumed the position of parade rest. Once the last note had sounded, members of the regimental color guard positioned alongside the flagpole fired a blank cartridge from a World War II pack howitzer, the report caroming off the kaserne's perimeter walls. Tubby came to attention and saluted. As the anonymous bugler played "To the Colors," three soldiers, under an NCO's watchful eye, lowered and folded the flag.

Since Tubby's earliest days as a cadet at West Point, this simple ceremony had never failed to move him. Someday, he silently reflected, he was going to miss it.

Once the ceremony concluded, he resumed his journey to the O-club, feeling a reluctance bordering on distaste. But further delay would not improve either the food or the club's hideous décor, with drapes, carpet, vinyl-covered dining room chairs all in clashing floral patterns. On the walls were framed prints of the Bavarian Alps. In one corner, several winking slot machines waited expectantly, along with an old upright piano that no one had played in years. Dominating the room was an oversized portrait of a black bird, painted by some anonymous artist of questionable talent.

Over the bar, a stenciled sign all-too-predictably designated the premises as the "Ravens' Roost."

Interspersed among shelves of liquor bottles were various gaudy tchotchkes, most of them promoting George Dickel Tennessee Whiskey. George D was the regiment's unofficial beverage of choice, consumed in copious quantities on convivial occasions, such as promotion parties and the 16th U.S. Cavalry's annual birthday bash.

Apart from a couple of young captains nuzzling their even younger dates—just looking at them made Tubby feel past his prime—the place was nearly empty. Seated at the bar was a single patron, a grizzled warrant officer still in uniform. CW3 Terry Ford—no relation to the commander-in-chief, as he tirelessly explained—was a master of all things automotive. He also possessed a herculean work ethic that he applied to his duties as maintenance officer of headquarters troop.

Ford had grown up in segregated Memphis and barely managed to finish high school. At age eighteen, on his father's urging, he had enlisted, chiefly to avoid the draft. It turned out to be a smart move. Rather than handing him a rifle, the Army trained him to be a mechanic. Under the hood, Ford found his life's work. In a succession of assignments, a knack for keeping aging vehicles in running order made him an invaluable asset and led to multiple promotions.

Terry Ford was never going to win prizes for good looks. A bad case of teenage acne had pitted his complexion. Now nearing forty, he had big ears to go with a beer belly and was just beginning to lose his hair. Grease and oil had permanently discolored his fingernails and chewing tobacco his teeth. Yet no one at Merrell Barracks put in longer hours, to include routinely working weekends.

Whenever he finally finished for the day, Ford headed straight to the club, usually still wearing stained army-issue coveralls. There, he laid claim to a seat at the far end of the bar, where he munched on pretzels, drank, and gossiped with anyone who cared to join him.

Although Ford and Tubby wore the same unit patch and occupied adjacent BOQ rooms, they rarely saw each other. Tubby seldom had occasion to visit the motor pool, and Ford went out of his way to avoid coming anywhere near regimental headquarters. As a consequence, they were no more than nodding acquaintances. Even so, lonely enough without Isabelle, Tubby sensed in Ford an even lonelier soul. Now, as he sidled past the bar toward the dining room, he touched Ford lightly on the elbow and spoke.

"Hey, Chief, how are you doing?"

Ford looked up, surprise on his face.

"Fine, Major, just fine," he said. "Join me for a drink?"

The invitation was unsought and unexpected, but Tubby saw no way to decline without being obviously rude.

"Sure. Not healthy for a man to drink alone."

"Oh, I don't know about that. I do it all the time."

He treated Tubby to a tightlipped smile.

"What'll you have?" Ford asked.

"George D and ginger will suit me just fine."

"Tommy!" Ford gestured with his right hand to catch the bartender's eye. "Two more Ravens Highballs."

"So, how are you doing, Chief?"

"Well, since you asked, not especially well."

The barkeep arrived with their drinks.

"Put them on my tab, Tommy," Ford said.

"You should let me get these," Tubby offered, raising his glass in a toast.

"Next round is yours."

"Fair enough. Now, fill me in on how life in the Kingdom of the Ravens is treating you."

"Well, I've stayed too effing long."

"You mean here at Merrell Barracks?"

"No, in the Army."

Ford sipped his drink.

"Mind if I smoke?" he asked.

"Not at all," Tubby said, and while resisting the temptation to mooch a cigarette, he noticed the wedding ring on Ford's left hand as he lit up.

"I had it all worked out, Major. I was going to finish my twenty and retire. Then, with my tidy little pension, I'd return to Tennessee to open an auto repair shop. Me and the missus would be set for life."

"What happened?"

"She got tired of waiting. Last fall, she left Memphis and took my kid with her. I don't know where they went. All I know is I'm here, busting my knuckles on beat-up old trucks and probably drinking too much."

"Why not take some leave and go find her?"

Ford chewed on Tubby's question.

"I guess because I can't face knowing why she left. Anyway, she'd just say it was my fault for being over here too long. And she might be right."

He picked up his drink and took another sip. Then, he put his cigarette to his mouth and inhaled.

"I dunno, Major. I don't mind the Army. In some ways, it's been good to me. But there's got to be more to life than this."

Before Tubby could ask Ford what he meant by more, he felt someone tapping on his shoulder. It was F.X., for once clothed in some semblance of civilian attire. Although still annoyed with his friend, Tubby grinned.

"Well," he said, "look what a cold wind out of the Czechoslovak Socialist Republic just blew in."

F.X. ignored the gibe.

"Might I interest the two of you in dinner?" he asked. "Note that I make no promises regarding quality."

"Not for me, Chaplain," Ford replied. "I've just finished the Sunday evening special—which I do not recommend. But you gentlemen go ahead. I'll stay here and nurse this fine beverage."

"Okay," Tubby said, "but I owe you a Ravens Highball."

"I won't forget, Major."

"See you, Chief. Come on, F.X., let's get some chow."

The dining room was now quite empty. As the pair sat down, Monika, the only waitress on duty, tossed a pair of cardboard coasters on the table and asked if they would be ordering drinks. She conveyed the ill-temper of someone unaccustomed to working late on Sunday nights. When Tubby hastily ordered a bottle of Riesling, she stomped off toward the bar. She was not in the mood to be placated.

Tubby broke the silence.

"My friend," he said, "I have a bone to pick with you."

"I'm sorry, Tubby," F.X. replied morosely. "I owe you an apology and an explanation."

"Yes, you certainly do. So, let's get it over with."

"I've spoken with Emma Meier since you saw her earlier today. Actually, I went to see her this afternoon, after my last mass."

"And?"

"So, you know that I'd been in touch with Sid Marks, both in my capacity as regimental chaplain and as a Catholic priest."

"Why the secrecy?"

"Privacy. Ethics. Seal of the confessional. Call it what you will. He came to me because he needed help. Once he began spilling his guts, I felt obliged to respect his confidence."

"Even after he killed himself?"

"His death didn't change any of that. Besides, I felt certain that once you began nosing around, you'd unearth as much of the story as I had. Which you have."

"Not quite. I've now read Sid's 201 file, but I still don't know what he saw or did in Vietnam that affected him so deeply."

"Well, okay, I'll tell you what I know. It's not pretty."

Monika returned with the wine, which she uncorked and poured, all without cracking a smile. F.X. consumed most of a glass before he resumed speaking. It was apparent to Tubby that his friend was ill at ease.

"Where were you in the spring of 1970, when we invaded Cambodia?" F.X. asked.

"At West Point, teaching Shakespeare to cadets."

"A good place to be. I was in-country, chaplain of a unit that led the charge into the Fishhook. This late in the War, our guys were not in a mood to play nice. Here, at last, was a chance to turn the tables and clean out NVA sanctuaries in supposedly neutral Cambodia."

"So said Nixon."

"Well, we certainly did that, but it was an ugly business."

Tubby listened quietly.

"Sid Marks," F.X. continued, "was a newbie, just assigned as a platoon leader in A Troop. This was his first major operation. There was a lot of contact. Marks says—Marks told me—that he witnessed a unit near his shooting up a Cambodian village pretty much for the hell of it."

Tubby winced.

"How many killed?" he asked.

"Two dozen, maybe three. Not a huge number by My Lai standards, but not trivial, either."

"And Marks did what?"

"That night, after bedding down his platoon, he reported to his troop commander—told him what he had seen. The CO warned Marks that tagging a sister unit with a war crime might not be a good career move. Even so, he agreed to pass the report up the chain. We don't know if that actually happened. We do know that, two days later, Sid was wounded and medevac'd to Japan. According to Sid, his report, if it existed, went nowhere."

"How did he know that?"

"Because the commander of the unit that shot up the village was Hugh Massey. He was there. He gave the orders. That's what Sid Marks told me."

"Is Massey aware of the accusations that Marks made in 1970?"

"Almost certainly not. Remember, Marks was in-country for only a matter of days. Massey probably never met him. May not have ever even laid eyes on him."

"Was Marks telling the truth? Did you believe him?"

"I believe that Sid Marks felt certain that he saw what he told me he saw. I also know, without a doubt, that he was a deeply troubled young man. Marks should not have been put in command of L Troop. He probably shouldn't have been in the Army at all."

"After reading his 201 file, I have to agree."

"And, Tubby, you know as well as I do why he got L Troop. Because the Lord of the Ravens wanted to send a message to Big Al: When it comes to racial equality, the 16th ACR is fully onboard. Putting Sid Marks in command of L Troop was the worst sort of tokenism."

Monika interrupted. Her mood had not improved in the intervening minutes. The kitchen, she told them, would soon be closing. Would they be wanting dinner? Less out of any enthusiasm for what the cook might conjure up than to shoo her away, they each ordered a cheeseburger with fries.

Lowering his voice, F.X. continued.

"From Sid's point of view, Massey is a murderer who got away with it—decorated, twice promoted, selected for a prestigious command. Then, the Fates intervene. Sid finds himself in a job he doesn't particularly want, working for someone he can't stand. And when a jeep accident caused Big Al's visit to the Kingdom of the Ravens to unravel, Massey wasted no time in fingering Marks himself as the scapegoat, with Quickdraw 6 quickly concurring."

"And?"

"The injustice of it all pushed Sid Marks over the edge. That's why he killed himself."

"In your opinion."

"Yes, in my opinion."

"Nice theory. Can you prove it?"

"No. I'm counting on you to do so—or to come up with a better explanation."

VI

Monday, 16 February

At Merrell Barracks, the morning fog was impenetrable and would take hours to burn off. The memorial service at Camp Rotz would have to wait until the weather permitted the RCO to fly, with the officers and men of L Troop obliged to adjust accordingly. Since time immemorial, armies had functioned this way: Hurry up, wait, and hope that those higher up would eventually show up or, better still, find something else to do.

Without giving the matter much thought—in Bavaria this time of year, fog was anything but unusual—Tubby made his own adjustment. He devoted the first several hours of the duty day to clearing an accumulation of notes and documents off his desk, intermittently listening to the headlines on AFN. The news from Stateside had the incumbent Gerald Ford, along with Ronald Reagan and Hubert Humphrey, all tied in the polls as likely presidential candidates.

Paperwork is the bane of an adjutant's existence. And with Lieutenant Colonel William Erskine, the regimental executive officer, off skiing in Garmisch with his latest girlfriend, Tubby was effectively doing double-duty. Not that Erskine — "call me Billy" — was of much help in even the best of circumstances. Having been passed over for further promotion after getting more than one less-than-perfect efficiency report, he was counting the days until he could retire, settle in Florida, and set himself up as a charter captain.

What made Tubby's de facto dual-hatting manageable was that he took neither position all that seriously. Crucially, he had developed an aptitude for sorting, a skill that he now put to use. In one pile went documents the RCO himself needed to see or sign. To some of these, he attached a brief handwritten recommendation, using notepaper embossed with the regimental crest. In another pile were papers that Tubby was farming out to members of the R-staff. In another still — the largest — were papers that he consigned to the trash.

Most importantly, he passed word to the RCO that next-of-kin notifications for Sergeant Borski's wife, living in a trailer outside of Fort Bliss, and for Specialist Cotton's parents, retired near Boise, had been completed. Efforts to identify Sid Marks' next of kin, on the other hand, had thus far come up empty.

Finally, a note from the ROC told him that an American claiming to be a reporter with the *New*

York Times had called, asking to speak to Colonel Caldwell. The reporter had left a name and phone number, along with the request that someone return his call.

At the bottom of Tubby's inbox was a thick document containing USAREUR's guidance for celebrating the upcoming bicentennial. He felt grateful that the RS3 had principal responsibility for implementing the directive. He cringed at the prospect of the fireworks, flag-waving, and patriotic speeches that would fill the regiment's calendar in early July. Was this an indication that the imprint of four years at West Point was wearing thin?

In truth, he had hated his four years as a cadet. But to quit and go home would have been humiliating and would have brought shame to his family, his parents in particular. They had been so proud when he was offered an appointment. In Bronzeville, going "out East" to attend a famous school had been a mark of real distinction.

Now, he had begun to wonder if attending the Academy had been a mistake. Certainly, the education he had received was not all it was cracked up to be. At the very least, it did not align with his own inclinations. The career path on which he found himself was fast losing whatever appeal it had once held. Perhaps, soldiering was just not for him. That subversive thought made him feel slightly uncomfortable. And yet, he also found it alluring.

By late morning, the weather was becoming flyable. Tubby and F.X. walked from the regimental headquarters to the RCO's helipad in the center of the kaserne's parade ground. The Lord of the

Ravens, meanwhile, chose to traverse the few hundred yards in his armored Mercedes.

As a source of clamorous noise in the center of a residential neighborhood, the helipad was a sore point with the local community. For Quickdraw 6, however, it was a cherished perk: one more tiny but pointed reminder of who had won World War II.

To distract himself from the helicopter's noise and headache-inducing exhaust, Tubby used the flight to Rotz to update the RCO on various matters. Prominent among them was the need to appoint a new commander for L Troop. Tubby handed Caldwell a list of a half dozen candidates, without getting a decision. He also suggested that the RCO set aside a few minutes after the ceremony to discuss the ongoing inquiry into the death of Sid Marks, with Hugh Massey and the regimental chaplain sitting in, as well. Caldwell gave his assent.

By the time the RCO entered the encampment at Rotz, several dozen members of L Troop had formed up on three sides of the flagpole. A plywood podium stood on the open side of the formation. Pawing the ground nearby was Hugh Massey, who had driven over from Amberg.

The event that followed was strikingly devoid of feeling. Lieutenant Thurlow, the acting troop commander, called the formation to attention. A recording of *The Star-Spangled Banner* played over loudspeakers. As squadron commander, Massey approached the podium and dutifully expressed regret about the tragic events of the prior week. Chaplain Scanlan came next. He recited a nondenominational, army-approved prayer that asked the Almighty to look favorably upon the souls of the departed.

Then, Caldwell stepped forward, removed a piece of paper from the breast pocket of his field jacket, and baffled those in attendance by launching into a poetic recitation:

> Chant this chant of my silent soul, in the name of all dead soldiers.
> Faces so pale, with wondrous eyes, very dear, gather closer yet;
> Phantoms, welcome, divine and tender!
> But sweet, ah sweet, are the dead, with their silent eyes.
> Dearest comrades! all now is over;
> But love is not over — and what love, O comrades!

This was not language to which the typical American soldier was accustomed. Even so, as the Lord of the Ravens stepped back from the podium, he looked rather pleased with himself.

"Walt Whitman," Tubby whispered to F.X.

A recording of "Taps" followed. Then, within twenty minutes, it was over. Of the speakers, only F.X. had mentioned the deceased by name. None had described the circumstances of their passing. When Thurlow dismissed the formation, the assembled soldiers, relieved to be done, shouted "Duty, with Honor, Sir!" and scattered.

Caldwell and Massey immediately headed to the troop commander's office, with Tubby and F.X. trailing behind. Long since scrubbed clean of any signs of prior occupancy, the office contained a standard Army desk and two standard Army office chairs. The walls were bare. Caldwell situated himself behind the desk and claimed one of the chairs. Massey sat down in the other. Tubby and F.X. remained standing.

"Okay, Tubby, what have you got for us?" the RCO asked.

"Not good news. It appears likely that Captain Marks killed himself as a delayed response to something that he witnessed—or claimed to have witnessed—in Vietnam."

"What did he witness?"

"An atrocity committed by U.S. forces during the Cambodian incursion."

Tubby eyed Hugh Massey, who remained impassive.

"I don't get the connection," Caldwell said.

Tubby drew a deep breath.

"Marks was a rookie platoon leader assigned to A Troop of the 17th Cav during the attack into the Fishhook. On approximately May 5, the unit adjacent to his—he says it was B Troop—assaulted a Cambodian village and killed a number of unarmed civilians. There were no NVA anywhere in sight. That's what Marks said, anyway. The B Troop commander was Captain Fitzhugh Massey."

Massey shot out of his chair.

"That's total bullshit," he erupted. "Marks was either lying or deluded."

"Okay, let's calm down," Caldwell said, motioning Massey to sit. "That's a mighty serious charge, Major. What's the evidence?"

"What we have is Marks' own account, given on separate occasions to his German girlfriend and to Chaplain Scanlan here. Nothing documented. There may also have been an official complaint lodged at the time of the alleged incident, but it's long gone."

"Chaplain?"

"Yes, that is essentially what Captain Marks told me."

"Colonel Massey?"

Massey was livid.

"B Troop did not intentionally kill civilians," he said vehemently. "Did we get in a fight on May 5? Probably. We were getting into firefights every day. And whatever we saw or did, I reported up the chain. Now, years later, we're supposed to take seriously the made-up story of someone who last week committed suicide by blowing his brains out, corroborated by some Fraulein who is probably a whore? I cannot believe this conversation is happening. Fucking bullshit."

Tubby spoke directly to the RCO.

"Look, Colonel, my job was to investigate. I don't claim to have reached definitive conclusions. But the information I just gave you has already leaked to the press. A *New York Times* reporter has shown up in Nurnberg, and he's eager to speak with you. This story is not going away."

"What are you suggesting?"

"For starters, I think you should give the corps commander a heads-up, and you should read your JAG into the situation. As your lawyer, he needs to know what's going on. It may also make sense for Lieutenant Colonel Massey to consult legal counsel.

If we do anything to suggest that we aren't taking these allegations seriously, harm to the regiment's reputation will be the least of the fallout."

"Chaplain, what's your take?"

"This sort of thing is way out of my lane, sir. But I think Major Hicks is probably right."

Hugh Massey threw up his hands and looked at the ceiling.

"That's it," he snarled. "I'm not putting up with any more of this crap."

He stormed out of the room, slamming the door behind him.

With that, the discussion ended. Projecting an air of mastery that he was not feeling, the Lord of the Ravens glanced at his Rolex.

"Time for me to get back to home station," he announced. "Tell the bird to crank."

•

Larry Kaplan did not consider himself a gourmand. Since taking up his current post, however, he had come to appreciate the delights of Fruhstuck, the simultaneously simple yet sumptuous breakfasts served in premier German hotels. He could not imagine a better way to start the day: crisp white linen tablecloths; a selection of freshly squeezed juices; the choice of strong dark coffee, or rich hot chocolate. And then, the vast array of foods displayed on the buffet table: sliced meats and cheeses, fresh berries and yogurt, pastries with butter, honey, and various preserves, along with pickled delicacies, cereal, and, of course, eggs. Recorded music—was it Mozart?—quietly playing in the background.

Since his boyhood in Pittsburgh, Larry had been partial to soft-boiled eggs, and that's what he chose this morning. Granted, the meal in its entirety was probably not good for his cholesterol. But what was life without at least some enjoyment? Divorced, in his mid-sixties, and finished with romance, he took inordinate pleasure from this first meal of the day. And, anyway, the *Times* was picking up the tab.

Zaid Muhammed arrived at Larry's table just as he had begun a second pot of coffee.

"Good morning, Mr. Muhammed. Please, sit down. Breakfast?"

"Just coffee. And call me Zaid."

"Excellent. Let me pour a cup. And I'm Larry."

The pleasantries disposed of, Larry Kaplan got to work. Pulling a pen and notebook from his jacket, he peppered Zaid with questions about the 16th ACR, its mission, its leadership, Sid Marks, Emma Maier, and anything and everything that might provide insight into the suicide. Zaid received a masterclass in journalistic thoroughness, free of charge.

"I definitely need to interview Emma Maier," Kaplan concluded. "And I'd like to speak with Colonels Caldwell and Massey, and also with Major Hicks. Can you arrange those?"

"Emma Maier, yes. We can see her today. Caldwell and Massey, unlikely. They won't want to talk to reporters. Hicks, perhaps. You should also consider the chaplain, Scanlan."

"Why not Caldwell and Massey?"

"Vietnam. You know better than I that senior officers took one lesson from the War: Nothing good can come from talking to the media. Whatever you may say, they will think your purpose is to humiliate them."

"Hicks is different?"

"Look, I don't know him well, but I think so. The War affected him differently than the others. I'm not sure why he's even in the Army. He doesn't fit."

•

The RCO used the flight back from Rotz to take stock. The situation was not playing out as he and Hugh Massey had intended. A change of plans was in order. That Massey himself might have to be sacrificed was emerging as a possibility. The thought of taking down the arrogant little prick did not cause Caldwell undue distress. If it could be done cleanly, the prospect had a certain appeal.

Yet, looming in the background was the possibility of Constance Massey making a difficult situation infinitely worse by involving her father. To avert that prospect, Caldwell needed Massey to remain an ally.

Caldwell's immediate concern, however, was to reduce his own vulnerability. A troubled young officer who he had placed in command had taken his own life. The imperative of the moment was to forestall any questions about his own judgment in giving Sid Marks L Troop. That had been his decision and his alone, and he did not want to be second guessed. With that in mind, establishing friendly relations with the woman who was carrying Marks' child had become a priority. A visit to convey his and the regiment's heartfelt condolences was in order.

Once back in the office, Caldwell phoned his wife, asking her to accompany him to Emma's apartment. Harriet, however, wasn't buying.

"Why is this my problem, Bart? A young woman foolishly allows herself to get pregnant without bothering to get married. Has she never heard of birth control?"

"Well, since you're the First Lady of the Regiment, I thought…"

Harriet interrupted before her husband could complete the sentence.

"Don't patronize me, Bart. It's your regiment, not mine, and she's not a member of it. She's not even American, for God's sake."

Referring to his wife as "First Lady" had been a monumental blunder. While Harriet conscientiously performed certain duties as a commander's spouse, she did not delude herself regarding her status. Women's roles were changing. Whatever standing had once accrued from being married to an Army colonel was fast disappearing. Harriet knew this, and she also knew that it was too late for her to seize the opportunities opening up to younger women. Even so, her willingness to defer to her husband's wishes had strict limits. Visiting Emma exceeded those limits.

"Feel free to go calling if you like, Bart, but I'm not up for handholding with strangers today."

After several decades of marriage, Caldwell knew that Harriet was not going to budge. So, after summoning the regimental chaplain and the armored Mercedes, he set off on his own. He felt little enthusiasm for the duty he was about to perform.

●

Larry Kaplan and Zaid Muhammed were just leaving Emma's apartment when Bart Caldwell arrived, F.X. in tow.

Zaid nodded to the priest.

"Good to see you again, Father."

Then, turning to Kaplan, he said:

"This is the regimental chaplain—friends with Major Hicks."

Kaplan ignored the introduction, giving his attention, instead, to the full colonel displaying a Ravens patch on his left shoulder. He pulled a card out of his pocket and thrust it at Caldwell.

"Larry Kaplan of the *Times*, Colonel, hoping to arrange an interview."

Caught off guard, Caldwell accepted the card then mumbled his reply.

"Call my adjutant," he said, "and we'll see."

His visit with Emma was not off to a great start.

Emma herself was already standing at the door. Her thin hair pulled back in a ponytail, she was wearing a pale blue maternity dress with a pattern of tiny, non-descript flowers. None of the uninvited guests parading through her apartment to talk about Sid had bothered to ask about her due date, but it was coming soon.

After motioning Caldwell and F.X. to enter, Emma wearily took a seat, clearly indifferent as to whether the two American soldiers stood or sat. The Lord of the Ravens spoke first.

"Fraulein Meier, I am Colonel Barton Caldwell, commander of the 16th Armored Cavalry Regiment."

"I know who you are," Emma said.

"I have come to express condolences on my own behalf and that of the regiment for the passing of your…for the passing of Captain Sydney Marks. I want you to know that we share your sadness. Captain Marks was a fine officer, and we will miss him."

Emma stared at him, skepticism written all over her face. Caldwell paused awkwardly and then plowed on.

"If there is anything we in the regiment can do for you, please, let us know. I am designating Chaplain Scanlan here to be the regimental point of contact. Please, don't hesitate to call on him as needed."

This was the first that F.X. had heard of this new assignment. In practical terms, there was little that the regiment, or even the entire U.S. Army, could do to ease Emma's predicament. From her own upbringing as the daughter of an absent G.I., she herself knew that. So did Caldwell. For help, Emma would have to rely on whatever her estranged mother and the German government could provide. Beyond that, she and her baby were on their own.

"Thank you," Emma replied, before lapsing into silence.

The ticking of a clock was the only sound in the apartment. F.X. came to the rescue.

"Fraulein," he said, "let me reinforce Colonel Caldwell's words. I knew that Sid was struggling, and I deeply regret my inability to help him. His passing is a terrible thing."

Here, F.X. was applying a lesson he had learned in the first year after his ordination: Offer solace but avoid making promises you can't fulfill.

"Please," he continued, "call me if can be of assistance. You already have my phone number at the chapel."

Sensing an opening, the RCO made a slight bow and backed toward the door. Without tripping over any furniture, he made his escape and headed directly to the Mercedes. As he settled into the backseat, he breathed an audible sigh of relief.

"Well, Chaplain," he said, "I thought that went pretty well."

"As good as it could have, sir," F.X. replied.

The lie came too easily, and he felt a stab of conscience. Through his seminary training and his years as a priest, he had learned to distinguish between good and evil. A fib to make the RCO feel good was a trivial matter—a venial sin, at most. Complicity in abandoning the mother of Sid Marks' child to her fate was not trivial. It was mortally sinful. F.X. resolved to right the wrong—or at least to make an attempt to do so.

"Sir, I wonder if I might have one more minute with Fraulein Meier—in my capacity as your designated point of contact. There's a question I need to ask her."

Caldwell looked at F.X. skeptically.

"All right, Chaplain, but make it quick."

F.X. shifted his considerable bulk out of the sedan and headed back toward the apartment. He entered without bothering to knock.

"Fraulein, please forgive this further intrusion, but can you give me your father's name?"

"Reggie Holt," she answered, a puzzled look on her face.

"Do you know where he was from in the States?"

"Ohio, I think. But I'm not sure."

"Reggie Holt. Thank you. I intend to find him. At least, I'll try. And if I do, I'll let him know that he's about to become a grandfather—and that he has responsibilities to you and to your baby."

As F.X. turned and walked back to the RCO's waiting car, Emma stared in disbelief.

●

Back in Amberg, snow was now steadily falling. The wind was picking up. Long past regular duty hours, Hugh Massey trudged across the compact kaserne, through the side gate, and back to his quarters. It had been a trying day.

After mulling the matter over for longer than it probably deserved, he had decided to pull L Troop off the border. Lion's rotation at Rotz was nearing its end, anyway, and given the trauma of the past few days, it could use a breather. Nor was Hugh comfortable in entrusting the 3rd Squadron border sector to the less than inspiring team of Thurlow and Chisholm for any longer than necessary. K Troop had a tested commander and a solid first sergeant, and it was next up in the rotation, anyway. Returning Lion to home station, giving the troops a couple days off, and prodding Caldwell to decide who would replace Marks seemed a sensible course of action. Without asking for the RCO's approval, he issued the necessary orders, reflecting with satisfaction that Caldwell would be annoyed that he had acted without getting formal approval. As far as Hugh Massey was concerned, it was his decision to make: He owned the 3rd Squadron sector.

As he entered his quarters, he felt the weight of responsibility melt away. It always felt good to come home. Tossing his mud-encrusted boots into the front hallway, he walked into the kitchen to give his wife a kiss—and to gauge how much refreshment she may have already consumed. Tonight, Con was in tolerably decent shape, which was good, since they needed to have a serious talk. He went upstairs to shower and change.

More than twenty years after they had first begun dating at West Point, Constance Massey remained the most remarkable woman Hugh had ever met. She exhibited a quiet single-mindedness that was a prerequisite for greatness. From his study of military history, Massey knew that Alexander the Great and Napoleon had possessed this quality. So, in entirely different forms, had Washington and

Grant. Perhaps, Patton or Ridgway, but no American officer since. How she had acquired it was a mystery.

Her gender denying her the opportunity to attend West Point, Connie had enrolled at age eighteen in Ladycliff, a small Catholic women's college located just outside West Point's main gate in Highland Falls, New York. Wags had it that Ladycliff existed to provide promising young brides for promising young Academy graduates. Although this was deeply unfair, in Connie's case, the slander contained a modicum of truth. She and Hugh met when he was a plebe and dated for four years—she lost her virginity as a sophomore during a weekend stay with Hugh at the New Yorker Hotel—and they married in the Cadet Chapel during June Week, just two days after his graduation.

She became a model Army wife, traveling from one post to the next and enduring prolonged separations. Had she married Hugh in the 1930s, she might have found fulfillment in this role. But, by the 1960s, amidst the furies released by Vietnam, being a model Army wife was losing whatever cachet it may once have possessed.

Connie needed something more. What she needed was for Hugh to make good on their shared ambitions and thereby justify the choices she had made as a young girl. With the passage of time, it had gradually dawned on her that she could have chosen a different path, one centered not on her husband's ambitions but on her own. This belated realization gnawed at her.

By the time Hugh came back downstairs, his hair still wet and uncombed, he had donned baggy brown corduroys and an orange sweater. On his feet were worn suede moccasins—West Pointers were seldom known for their fashion sense. He found Connie in the kitchen, mixing herself a drink. She asked Hugh if he would join her.

"Not now, Con, perhaps in a bit."

The Masseys' twin daughters, fifth-graders oblivious to the darkness overshadowing their mother's life, had already finished dinner, and were now in the backroom, mesmerized by a mindless TV program. Their parents could talk without fear of interruption.

"We've got big trouble," Hugh began, speaking very quietly. "The Marks suicide is about to become national news back home, and I'm likely to be tagged as the fall guy."

He recounted the conversation involving Tubby and the RCO earlier that day at Rotz.

"Is it true, Hugh? Were you involved in war crimes?"

"How can you even suggest that? Of course, not!"

Massey's raised voice prompted the girls to look up, but only briefly. *The Partridge Family*—one of several cancelled sitcoms that had found a second life on AFN—quickly recaptured their attention.

"Well, then, let me call my father," Connie whispered. "He'll know how to handle this."

"Don't even think of it. That would only make things worse. Once involve him and this whole thing is out of our hands."

"What, then?"

"I'd like you to check in with Tubby Hicks, my classmate and supposed friend. As soon as possible. He and that priest set this whole screwed-up mess in motion by taking Marks' wild charges seriously. I don't pretend to understand Tubby's game, but he may be able to help us."

"What should I ask him?"

"Why does he consider Marks to be credible? Why take his allegations seriously? It's ridiculous."

"Okay. I'll talk to him."

"Thanks, darling. One thing's for sure: If I go down, I'm not going alone."

"If *we* go down, you mean. I was going into Nurnberg tomorrow, anyway. I need to get some things at the PX and swing by the Class VI store. I'll ask Tubby to meet for lunch. He never says no to me."

VII

Tuesday, 17 February

By morning, the snow had stopped, and the wind had eased. A fresh blanket of white, several inches deep, covered the Land of the Ravens from the regimental headquarters to the most remote border outpost. On days like this, unless you happened to be a soldier, you looked for excuses to stay in bed. If you were a soldier, duty called, and it was likely to involve the extensive use of brooms and shovels.

For the RCO, the first duty of the day was one he dreaded: placing a call to his immediate boss, the VII Corps commander. Caldwell had worked for Lieutenant General Willard G. O'Malley just long enough to know that he had an acute antipathy toward bad news. Anything that embarrassed his corps embarrassed him personally. He would, therefore, interpret untoward publicity stemming from the suicide of Captain Sydney Marks as a personal affront. Who to blame—he was himself not given to shouldering personal responsibility when things went awry—would become an instant priority. Staying clear of the line of fire was going to require a nimbleness that was not a Caldwell strength.

From his office, the RCO dialed the corps headquarters in Stuttgart. General O'Malley was busy at the moment, his secretary said in heavily accented English. Could Colonel Caldwell hold? Of course. Several minutes passed. Bart felt like he was sitting in a vice-principal's outer office, waiting to have his hand slapped.

O'Malley finally picked up.

"Is this Quickdraw 6?"

The corps commander enjoyed poking fun at subordinates who adopted colorful handles. He also prided himself on his ability to spot a phony. As a World War II draftee, he had never graduated from college. Deflating the pretensions of anyone inclined to put on airs was his idea of sport.

"Yessir, Bart Caldwell here. Hoping to brief you on a fairly sensitive matter that we have unfolding in the regiment."

"Okay, shoot."

Beginning with the Sid Marks suicide and its possible cause, Caldwell talked O'Malley through the entire sequence of events, concluding with Larry Kaplan's arrival on the scene and the prospect of an unfavorable *New York Times* story appearing in the coming days. O'Malley listened quietly until Caldwell had finished. Then, he dropped the hammer.

"Sounds like you've got a helluva problem on your hands, Bart. What are you proposing to do?"

Bart Caldwell had not prepared an answer to that particular question. In an instant, the Lord of the Ravens realized that he was flying solo.

"I understand, Boss. I own this one."

●

Tubby had accepted Connie Massey's invitation for lunch, knowing that she had more in mind than simply catching up with an old friend. Borrowing F.X.'s well-used Opel—its signature, a dented right-rear fender—he drove through the sloppy streets of Nurnberg, arriving just after noon at the several nondescript buildings comprising the PX complex.

Except when needing a haircut, Tubby studiously avoided the place. It was the worst of America transplanted to Bavaria. The massive parking lot with dirty snow piled up at the far end, the oversized steel carts with wheels that squealed, the shelves bulging with merchandise, and the crowds elbowing their way toward the checkout counter: It reminded him of everything he disliked about his shopping-obsessed countrymen.

When he walked into the snack bar, probably the most disagreeable eating establishment within a twenty-five-kilometer radius, Constance Massey was already seated at a table. Truth to tell, Connie loved the Nurnberg PX, snack bar included. While the 3rd Squadron's home station at Pond Barracks offered the soldiers and their families basic amenities, everything was small—where small meant dreary and inadequate. Life in Pond Barracks did not differ appreciably from daily existence in Warsaw or East Berlin. By comparison, a visit to the Nurnberg PX implied choice, perhaps even the possibility of finding on the clothing racks something a woman might actually wear.

"You look lovely, as always, Con."

Connie blushed. In truth, in anticipation of her lunch with Tubby, she had spent extra time on her hair and makeup. She looked very smart, in a powder blue ski jacket and designer jeans tucked inside suede boots, with a headband pulling back her blonde hair. Going as far back as Connie's days at Ladycliff, more than a few of the women in her circle, almost all of them white, had harbored a secret crush on Tubby. Connie herself had not been immune.

Tubby sat down and pretended to read the menu.

"The specials today are bad and worse. Which will you be having, my dear?"

"Oh, Tubby, I'll settle for a BLT and chips. And iced tea."

"Good enough for me."

He ordered for them both. Neither was looking forward to addressing the actual purpose of their meeting. So, they tacitly agreed to delay it.

"How are the girls?" Tubby asked.

"Oh, they're fine. Our little on-post school in Amberg is lousy, but they'll survive. They're not big on school, anyway."

"Well, they're still young."

"And how is Isabelle?"

Connie was asking out of courtesy. She barely knew Isabelle, having met her only once, at Tubby's wedding in Chicago. Apart from Tubby himself, the two women had nothing in common.

"You can't have heard the news. She lost the baby, Con."

"That's awful."

Connie reached across the table and covered his hand with hers.

"I'm very sorry."

"But she's okay. Already back at work. We'll get through this."

"Will you give her my best?"

"Of course. Thank you."

The brief exchange had exhausted his appetite for small talk. Carefully removing his hand from beneath hers, he leaned forward.

"Now, how about telling me the purpose of our rendezvous."

If the abrupt shift in tone bothered Connie, she concealed it.

"It's Hugh and this situation with Captain Marks, Tubby. It has us both very worried. I was hoping that you could give me some sense of what will happen from here."

The question was not unexpected.

"The honest answer is that I don't know."

"Don't know, or won't say?"

"Mostly don't know. A lot hinges on this guy Larry Kaplan. He's here reporting on the Marks story for the *Times.* More accurately, he's poking around to see if there *is* a Marks story."

"If there is?"

"If Kaplan concludes that Sid Marks killed himself because he was haunted by a war crime, the *Times* may choose to give it a lot of play. Then, the rest of the media will pile on. That will attract congressional attention—remember, back home, it's an election year."

"Damned politicians."

Tubby looked at her quizzically then continued.

"The Army will launch an inquiry, which will last for months and undoubtedly touch on other matters totally unrelated to what happened last week at Camp Rotz. All that is speculative on my part, but plausible."

"Where will that leave Hugh?"

"Hard to say. Things could get pretty nasty."

He hesitated for a moment to allow Connie to measure the import of his words.

"Worst case, he'll be charged with murder and court martialed. Best case, he'll have his reputation destroyed and his career effectively ended. And he won't be the only one hauled into the dock. Colonel Caldwell will be asked to explain why, among the several captains waiting for command, he moved Sid Marks to the front of the line. There could be more than a few collateral casualties."

Tears were welling up in Connie's eyes.

"I'm sorry, Con. I thought it best to give it to you straight."

"You're saying everything turns on this journalist."

"Maybe not everything, but a lot. Hugh wants this to go away. So does the RCO. I suppose I do, too."

She had begun to cry.

"If Kaplan decides that there's no story here worth his paper's attention, then Sid Marks' suicide won't get much play Stateside. And the whole question of what might have occurred in Cambodia will disappear. So, yes, a lot turns on Kaplan."

"So, what should we do?"

"That's for you and Hugh to decide. At West Point, they made a big deal out of telling the truth. That might be good advice here."

Although Tubby spoke calmly and even gently, his words left Connie feeling like she might faint. What she was expecting of Tubby was not entirely clear, even in her own mind. But it was more than reciting the Cadet Honor Code.

She suddenly felt an overwhelming desire to flee.

"I need to go."

Not waiting for her lunch to arrive, Connie collected her parcels and got up. Then, after steadying herself, she left without saying another word. She needed a drink.

●

As Tubby's lunch with Constance Massey was ending, Larry Kaplan was hunched over the wheel of a rented BMW, heading toward the 3rd Squadron headquarters in Amberg. He was not a very good driver and navigating the autobahn with cars whizzing past at very high rates of speed always put him on edge.

With assurances that the *Times* would compensate him for his efforts, Zaid had agreed to accompany Larry Kaplan as navigator and second set of eyes. The purpose of the outing was to cajole Hugh Massey into sitting for an interview. While this was probably a long shot, Kaplan figured that just nosing around the unit Massey commanded might turn up useful background related to the fate of Sid Marks.

For all their differences, Larry saw in Zaid something of himself when he was just starting out in the newspaper business. He was brash, scrappy, and unencumbered by manners.

Now, as they drove toward Amberg, Zaid was peppering Larry with questions completely divorced from the Sid Marks suicide.

Kaplan was Jewish? Yes. So, he was a big supporter of Israel?

"I'm an American. I wish Israel well, but I know which team I'm on."

"Well, my birth certificate says I'm an American. But that don't mean squat. Let me ask you: You Jews have done pretty well in America, while we Blacks have been screwed. How do you explain that?"

Kaplan shrugged.

"It's complicated."

"Racism isn't complicated."

"But times change, my friend. Not so long ago, even in the U.S., Jews were outsiders looking in.

Now, some crazies complain that we secretly run the whole damn country."

"It's different with us. White people will never allow my kind a seat at the table. Not willingly, anyway."

From what Larry Kaplan had seen in his years as a working journalist, he found it hard to disagree.

Zaid changed the subject.

"Tell me: Why drive to some little Bavarian burg on a crappy day in the middle of winter? What story are we after?"

Larry took note of the *we,* which he did not dispute.

"What story do *you* think we're after?"

"Me? Showing how the Army fucked over my Black brother."

"Sticking it to the Man."

"Yeah—something like that."

Zaid had spoken with evident heat.

"A perfectly legitimate angle," Kaplan said, "but not exactly a fresh one."

"And you have something better?"

"I'm not sure, but I think so. Maybe."

"Okay, lay it out."

"Look, your feelings about the Army differ from mine. We served in very different times. Do I feel any affection for the Army? No. But, perhaps, some empathy. This much I know: By sending it off to fight a really shitty war in Vietnam, the nation subjected American soldiers to big-time abuse—not altogether different from the way it abuses Black people."

"A bullshit comparison."

Larry ignored the remark and continued.

"The War totally fucked up the Army. So, now, it's trying to get itself unfucked. That means it has to become something other than what it was back when you were drafted. Whether it will succeed is a big question. *That*'s the story that interests me. And I think the answer is to be found in places like Amberg, where the everyday Army does its everyday thing."

"The Army is not my problem. I don't much care if it ever recovers."

"You don't have to. But absent some larger context, don't expect anyone to care about why Sid Marks killed himself."

●

Amberg is a small, walled city known—to the extent that it is known at all—for its several imposing gates and for an even larger number of excellent breweries. It lies well off the beaten track. Few tourists stop by, and fewer still stay longer than a couple hours.

Located outside the walls but within walking distance of the city center, Pond Barracks was another former Wehrmacht installation, long since appropriated for use by U.S. forces. A low wall surrounding the kaserne discouraged trespassers but possessed negligible defensive value. Inside the wall was a rectangular parade ground. On one end was the squadron headquarters, on the other the mess hall, with four-story tile-roofed barracks lining each side, everything painted a dull ochre. A clock-bearing cupola atop the mess hall was the sole concession to ornamentation. Off to the rear were maintenance facilities and motor pools, with tanks, trucks, and howitzers lined up in neat ranks. Taken as a whole, the place possessed all the charm of a school for farm equipment repair attended by wayward boys.

The battalion-sized element of U.S. troops stationed in Amberg comprised the entirety of U.S. combat power across a broad swathe of rural Bavaria. Yet, as a statement of policy and purpose, the garrison was largely symbolic, expressing inertia as much as intent. G.I.'s had been occupying Pond Barracks for decades. Their presence had become part of the natural order of things. Both the local German population and the U.S. troops rotating through on two-or-three-year tours of duty assumed that the squadron would remain fixed in place indefinitely.

The moviemaker John Ford might have used the kaserne as the backdrop for a nostalgic frontier saga, with armored vehicles standing in for horses. As a practical matter, however, the Army of the mid-1970s could ill-afford to indulge in nostalgia, and the 3rd Squadron of the 16th Armored Cavalry Regiment was no exception.

By 1976, the U.S. Army was shedding the last of its draftees and laboring to convert itself into a volunteer force—this at a time when Vietnam had soured many young Americans on the very idea of military service. So, the variously motivated—sometimes minimally motivated—soldiers who ended up in Pond Barracks were not necessarily the cream of their generation. It fell to commanders like Hugh Massey to mold them into a disciplined and cohesive fighting force. He welcomed the challenge.

After a couple of missed turns, Larry and Zaid arrived at the kaserne's front gate. A less than fully alert-looking sentry asked what their business might be. Larry Kaplan identified himself as a reporter from the *New York Times* hoping to see Lieutenant Colonel Massey. As far as the sentry was concerned, this was akin to requesting an audience with the Pope. Now fully awake, he hurriedly telephoned the squadron ops center for instructions. Direct the visitor to the squadron headquarters came the surprising reply.

Larry and Zaid drove the short distance to the building that the sentry had pointed out, parking in a spot marked "VIPS Only." A very senior NCO waited to greet them. Tall, well-built, Black, and accustomed to exercising authority, he was Command Sergeant Major Johnny Moultrie.

"Please, follow me," he commanded, eyeing Zaid suspiciously. From Moultrie's perspective, any Black male sporting an Afro was, at the very least, anti-American and, more than likely, an outright traitor.

At the end of the ground-floor hallway was the squadron commander's well-appointed office, adorned with plaques, Ravens paraphernalia, and autographed black-and-white portraits of various high-ranking officers, testifying to the exalted status of the office's principal occupant. Prominently displayed in this gallery was a photograph of Hugh Massey's father-in-law.

Massey himself rose from behind his desk to greet his visitors and invited them to sit at a well-polished conference table. Introductions, pleasantries—"How was the traffic coming down from Nurnberg?"—and offers of coffee followed.

Then, he got down to business.

"I'm sure that you gentlemen won't mind if my sergeant major sits in on our discussion."

Massey motioned for Johnny Moultrie to join them. The gesture conveyed a sense of complete ease in his surroundings. Hugh Massey was in his element. He was the absolute master of his realm.

"Now, what can I do for you?"

"My associate, Mr. Muhammed," Larry replied, with a nod toward Zaid, "and I are working on a story centered on the suicide of Captain Sydney Marks. We'd like to get your perspective on what happened and why."

"What ground rules?"

"Ground rules?"

"On the record? Off the record? On background?"

"What are your preferences, Colonel?"

"On background. I'll give you everything I know. And probably more than you want."

"All right, on background. No quotes. No attribution."

"Okay. For starters, Captain Marks should never have been given command of L Troop. There were other more deserving captains here in the squadron and elsewhere in the regiment who had been waiting longer. Marks was not ready. I'm not sure if he was ever going to be ready."

Larry interrupted.

"So, why did he get the job?"

"Caldwell made the decision. It's the RCO's prerogative to fill command positions. He ignored my recommendation and gave L Troop to Marks."

"Why?"

"Ask Caldwell. But my guess is Marks got the job because he was Black. He was the only Black captain in the regiment and Caldwell wanted to send a signal."

"What sort of signal?"

"That he has gotten the message from on high: Unless the Army shows that it is fully committed to racial equality, the all-volunteer experiment will fail."

"You disagree with that?"

"Not at all. I'm all for equal opportunity. JM here will testify to that."

"One hundred percent," the Sergeant Major affirmed.

"But one of my own guys here in the squadron has been waiting longer and is ready. Putting unqualified people in jobs they can't handle benefits no one. That's what happened in this instance. You want to blame someone for Marks committing suicide? Caldwell is your man."

Larry pivoted to the central question.

"Before he killed himself, Marks told people that you were directly involved in the murder of civilians in Cambodia."

"He lied. I am not a war criminal."

Zaid interrupted.

"So, why would Marks say such a thing?"

Hugh shot him a scornful look.

"Am I supposed to be a mind-reader? How would I know?"

He turned back to Larry Kaplan.

"Mr. Kaplan, did you serve?"

"Yes. 112th Infantry, 28th Division, here in Europe from '44 to '45."

"See any dead civilians?"

"Yes, quite a few."

"How about you, JM? You were in Korea at the very beginning. Did you see any dead civilians?"

"Yessir. Refugees fleeing south, slaughtered in great numbers. I'll never forget."

"Who pulled the triggers?"

"We did. Or, more precisely, it was mostly our pilots who did. They told us Reds were hiding among the refugees as a way to infiltrate into the South. That made any gook on two legs a legitimate target."

"Anyone get court-martialed as a result?"

"Not that I ever heard."

"Civilians get killed in every war, Mr. Kaplan. Probably more civilians than soldiers, in many cases. Between bombs dropped, poisons spread, and artillery shells randomly fired, God alone knows how many civilians we killed in Vietnam."

Hugh stopped, as if to organize his thoughts.

"No American has been held accountable for all those deaths—none. None will be. No president, no defense secretary, no member of Congress, no field commander. So, now, right out of the blue, you're going to write a story that singles me out as a murderer based on unsubstantiated accusations by a dead man?"

Larry raised his hand, as if to object, but Hugh Massey continued.

"If you do, here's what's going to happen. First, my own career will be destroyed. Apart from my wife, no one will care. Second, I will use my court martial—which I will demand—to put the crime I am charged with committing in a wider perspective. I will draw attention to all the civilians killed, maimed, and displaced as a direct consequence of our policies."

Although Larry Kaplan opened his mouth to speak, Massey continued, raising his voice a notch.

"My own testimony will elicit similar stories from other remorseful veterans. And, maybe, some who just want to enjoy a moment of notoriety. There will be many horrific accounts for your newspaper to feast on."

"The *Times* does not feast on horror," the reporter interjected.

Massey ignored the remark.

"Third, as a consequence, the Army's efforts to move beyond Vietnam and restore itself to some semblance of health will be set back a decade. After all, who would want to enlist in an organization mired in continuing scandal and charges of criminality? I wouldn't."

Hugh Massey looked at Larry and Zaid with contempt.

"So, please understand the full implications of what you are about to undertake. And now, gentlemen, this interview has ended. Have a safe drive back to Nurnberg. Sergeant Major, please see our guests out."

●

Tubby stayed at the PX long enough to finish his sandwich and then drove to the regimental chapel. He returned the Opel to F.X.'s reserved parking spot and walked inside to drop off the keys in his office. His friend was out, so he scrawled a brief note: *"Padre: Lunch with CM did not go well. If you're free, let's have dinner at Ingrid's. Meet at my Q at 6:30?"*

After scrawling his initials, he walked back to his own office, reflecting on his exchange with Connie. He had meant to be honest. Perhaps, he had been cruel. Certainly, he had upset her.

Within an hour, a livid Hugh Massey was calling him from Amberg.

"What the hell did you say to my wife, Hicks!"

"Ease off, Colonel. She wanted my take on the Marks situation. I told her that you were in real jeopardy, which is what I believe. And you're not the only one."

"Who invited you to butt in?"

"Con asked to see me. I'm guessing you knew that. She's a friend, so I agreed. I wasn't going to lie to her. And I won't lie to you. You're in deep shit."

Massey interrupted angrily.

"Stay out of my affairs, Major, and stay away from my wife."

The phone line went dead.

Whenever the RCO was away, quiet descended on the regimental headquarters. Today, Caldwell was off visiting 1st Squadron in Bindlach, giving the staff time to catch up on routine work and to start preparing for what was to come next. There were always events to plan for: training exercises, briefings, rehearsals, inspections, ceremonies, and visits by VIPs. The approaching Bicentennial added an extra layer of busyness.

Ordinarily, Tubby would have seized the opportunity to read, but today, he found himself too distracted. His encounter with Constance Massey left him with a sense of regret that he could not shake. A knock on the door disrupted his reflections. It was Sergeant Edwards from the ROC.

"What's up, Ezra?"

"Some reporter named Kaplan is on the phone asking to speak with the RCO. He's already called several times. What should I tell him?

"Put him through to me."

Moments later, the phone on his desk rang.

"Mr. Kaplan, this is Major Hicks, regimental adjutant, what can I do for you?"

Tubby listened as Larry Kaplan explained his hopes of interviewing Colonel Caldwell regarding the suicide of Captain Sydney Marks.

"Colonel Caldwell is away. But I will be sure to pass along your request when he returns."

Might Major Hicks himself be available for an interview?

"I'm tied up at the moment, Mr. Kaplan. But if you're free this evening, meet me at seven at the Goldener Fuss. It's a small gasthaus not far from the kaserne. Your colleague Herr Muhammed knows where it is."

Kaplan accepted the invitation and hung up.

Tubby was almost immediately assaulted by second thoughts. Why had he agreed to an after-hours meeting with Larry Kaplan? Mostly remorse, he supposed. He had told Constance Massey that the *Times* reporter posed a grave threat to her husband. Now, he felt an obligation to avert or at least lessen that threat. Sitting down with any reporter was a risky proposition. But, in this instance, the risk might be worth it.

●

It was already getting late when Tubby got back to his BOQ. To arrive at Ingrid's on time, he needed to hustle. As he was pulling off his uniform, he heard a knock.

"It's unlocked."

It was F.X., already having exchanged his fatigues for clerical threads.

"You coming?" Tubby asked.

F.X. nodded.

"Good. The *Times* reporter who's been nosing around is joining us. Probably that Muhammed character, too."

Tubby threw his fatigues on the bed and grabbed some clothes out of his closet.

"Okay, let me read you into something else," F.X. said as Tubby changed. "It's about Emma. The RCO wants me to do what I can for her. I've decided to take his order seriously, so I'm trying to locate her father. Some guy named Holt, who probably lives near Columbus, Ohio. His daughter needs help—it's time for Mr. Holt to become a real parent."

"Anything I can do?"

"No, it will take forever to get an answer through official channels. My fellow chaplains back in the States can locate Mr. Holt more quickly."

"Probably true."

Tubby's mind was elsewhere. He checked his look in the mirror and nodded. They were out the door and into the frosty Bavarian winter.

●

As Tubby had expected, Larry Kaplan brought along Zaid. Ingrid had seated them at a quiet table for four before Tubby and F.X. arrived. Larry was nursing an excellent Rheinhessen, Zaid a glass of Spetzi. Both were perusing a menu. Without being asked, Ingrid brought two beers.

"It's good of you to come, Major Hicks," Kaplan said. "And you, as well, Father Scanlan."

In no mood for chitchat, Tubby got down to business.

"Mr. Kaplan, it's the suicide of Captain Sydney Marks that brings you to Nurnberg. How's your story shaping up?"

Tubby's bluntness caught Larry off guard.

"The story has no shape. It's not even a story yet. I'm still gathering facts."

"Help me understand exactly what you are looking for."

Kaplan ignored the prosecutorial tone.

"Frankly, I was hoping that a conversation with you and Father Scanlan here might provide an answer to that very question."

"But why is this a matter of interest to the nation's paper of record? Suicides are commonplace. Even in the Army, they aren't exactly rare."

"Come on, Major, you're being coy. First of all, the 16th ACR is not an ordinary unit. It patrols the border with Communist Czechoslovakia. Second, Captain Marks was not an ordinary captain. He was a Vietnam veteran and, if I am not mistaken, the only Black officer to hold a command position in your entire regiment. And third, prior to his death, he had made allegations of a war crime committed several years ago by his immediate superior. A *Times* reader offered that bare recitation of facts would say: 'Tell me more.'"

"And don't forget the daughter of a former G.I. who is carrying Marks' baby," Zaid added. "Human interest bonus."

"So," Tubby said, "it sounds like you *do* have your story."

"The makings of a story, perhaps," Kaplan replied, "but I'm in no hurry. Tell me, Major, you have a reputation for honesty: Where are you on this? Off the record, if you like."

Ingrid approached the table.

"Gentlemen, if you wish to eat, please order now."

It was a command, not a request. When she had recorded their selections and departed for the kitchen, Tubby replied.

"Okay, off the record. I don't claim to have known Sid Marks well. Although we can speculate as to his why he killed himself, we don't know and will probably never really know."

Tubby withheld any reference to a suicide note, disregarding his advice to Connie to come clean.

"Granted, there's evidence to suggest that his tour in Vietnam scarred him badly. But that applies to any number of vets."

"True enough," Kaplan said.

"Why was Marks given command of L Troop? You'll have to take that up with Colonel Caldwell. It was his call, and I won't second-guess him."

"I wouldn't expect you to. But where do you come down on the larger question? Is there something here that the *Times* should be pursuing?"

"Well, what I see is this: You lack concrete evidence. And publication of a story based on speculation and innuendo is likely to hurt people I care about. It's also likely to damage the reputation of my regiment, if not the Army as a whole. I don't want to see any of that happen."

"That's understandable. And you think my friend Zaid and I are taking things in the wrong direction?"

"Candidly, yes."

"Let me ask you this, Major. The CID must have investigated this incident. Have you seen their report?"

"No, it went directly to Colonel Caldwell. And any findings will only be preliminary."

"I'd like to know more about the accident that occurred the day prior to Captain Marks killing himself."

"Almost certainly, the soldiers involved were driving too fast, and the one jeep flipped. It happens all too often."

"But why were they driving too fast? What was the hurry? My friend Zaid here has a theory."

"More than a theory," Zaid said. "More like fact-based speculation."

"Let's hear it," Tubby replied.

"It's hardly a secret that Czech-West German border security is piss-poor. After all, it's thickly forested and there's no wall—just a fence with a few strands of barbed wire, guarded by Czech conscripts not known for their fealty to the Kremlin. Through that fence passes all sorts of contraband: cigarettes, whiskey, luxury items you can't get in the East, but also Bibles and hymnals sent from church groups in the U.S."

"West German and Bavarian border police routinely patrol that border," Tubby interjected.

"True, but smuggling is like drunk driving," Zaid continued. "Put out enough patrols, and you might be able to reduce it, but you can't prevent it. I might even suggest that smuggling with the Czechs serves Western interests. Biblical subversion."

"So, what are you suggesting? That the L Troop patrol was engaged in illegal activity?"

"No, more likely they stumbled on a smuggling operation in progress and foolishly gave chase. As we used to say back in Valdosta: They were fucking around. Then, things took a bad turn, and two G.I.s ended up dead."

"When I talked to Wells and Hubbs, they said nothing remotely like this. And they were there."

"Exactly. Spilling the real story might get them in big trouble."

"What real story?"

"We don't know," Kaplan said. "That's what we're trying to find out. But once the CID had read them their rights, they'd be more likely to come clean."

"But if anything remotely like this had occurred," Tubby replied, "the CID would have informed Colonel Caldwell. He'd have your 'real story.'"

Zaid shrugged. Larry spoke up.

"We don't know what your Colonel Caldwell knows or doesn't know. We haven't been able to interview him. But it would be very interesting to have a look at what Wells and Hubbs told the CID. That might help me decide if there actually is a story here or not."

Steaming plates loaded with sausage, schnitzel, and buttery spaetzle were arriving.

"Ingrid, zwei bier, bitte," F.X. said. "And another Spezi for Herr Muhammed here."

After sampling his dinner, which met with his full approval, Kaplan continued.

"Major, I hope you don't mind my saying that your inquiry into this matter has been pretty superficial. Why Captain Marks killed himself is an interesting question that we may never be able to answer. But hovering in the background are other questions."

"Like what, for instance?"

"How well your regiment is performing its border mission, for one. What that performance says about the Army's ability to get its act together after Vietnam is another. From where I sit, the outlook isn't very promising."

F.X. had contributed nothing to this entire exchange. Now, he intervened to hijack the conversation. Kaplan turned out to be as passionate about the Pirates as F.X. was about the Cubs. In between bites, they began comparing notes on the coming National League race. Zaid rolled his eyes. Tubby wondered if there was something else his friend wasn't telling him.

●

When they returned from Ingrid's, F.X. insisted that he and Tubby stop by the ROC. An Ohio National Guard chaplain from near Columbus had left a message which included a name, address, and home phone number of Emma Maier's likely father. His name was Reginald D. Holt. It was late afternoon Eastern time back in the States, so F.X. immediately placed a call through the USAEUR switchboard to Holt's number, citing the RCO as his authority to do so.

When a woman answered, F.X. identified himself as a U.S. Army chaplain and asked if Reginald Holt might be available. No, he was not, and wouldn't be. The woman was obviously Holt's wife and showed no inclination to cooperate—or even to bring her husband to the phone.

As quickly as he could, F.X. explained the reason for the call. The woman was unmoved.

"More than twenty years ago, my husband made a mistake, which he regrets. Now, this girl, who you say is his daughter, is having difficulties. I am sorry for her. I truly am. But she is *not* a member of this family. We have enough trouble getting by just as it is. My husband works for the post office. Do you have any idea how much he makes?"

Not much, F.X. imagined, but he made one last effort to press his case. Would Mrs. Holt at least allow him to speak to her husband? No, she would not. Instead, she hung up. He listened for a moment to the dial tone. It was a rebuke, chastising the priest for inserting himself without invitation into the lives of strangers.

Without another word, F.X. replaced the phone in its cradle and abruptly walked out of the ROC, into the night's darkness. He fished his Zippo and a pack of Marlboros out of his overcoat and fired up a cigarette. Tubby had followed wordlessly. He could not recall ever having seen his friend so beside himself with righteous anger. He waited for the priest to speak.

When F.X. had finished his cigarette, he crushed the butt under the heel of his boot and took a deep breath.

"One thing's for certain. We now know who runs the Holt household, and it's not our man, Reggie. I guess we shouldn't be surprised. The SOB showed his true colors twenty years ago, back when he left Emma's mom in the lurch."

"So, now what?" Tubby asked.

"As much as it pains me to admit, Herr Muhammed was right: The Army won't be lifting a finger to help Emma. Regulations don't require and won't allow expending U.S. government resources on behalf of a pregnant girlfriend of a deceased soldier. But whether sincerely or not, the Lord of the Ravens says he wants something done unofficially on Emma's behalf. Those are my orders, and I'm not giving up just yet."

"What do you propose?"

"Mustering all the prestige accorded to me as regimental chaplain, I'm going to call on Emma's mom. And I'm going to enlist our friend Zaid to help. I want to see if the two of us can soften that hard heart of hers."

Tubby smiled.

"If today you hear His voice, harden not your hearts."

"Very *good*, Major. *Hebrews,* Chapter 3. The good nuns taught you well. We'll make a believer out of you yet."

VIII

Wednesday, 18 February

Quickdraw 6 knew exactly what the CID report said. Army investigators had provided him with a copy as soon as they had completed it. He had read it carefully then tucked it away in his desk for safekeeping. He had discussed its contents with no one, not even his wife.

The proximate cause of the accident was precisely what his adjutant had suspected in the first place: reckless behavior by soldiers assigned to his regiment. Or, in his preferred alternative framing: soldiers wearing the Ravens patch but under the direct and immediate command of Captain Sydney Marks. In accordance with accepted practice, the buck would stop there.

Ancient tradition has it that commanders are responsible for everything that occurs within their jurisdiction. In theory, this tradition is clearcut. Like the Ten Commandments, it does not allow for exceptions. When translating theory into practice, however, what appeared clearcut becomes much less so. As a practical matter, rank attenuates the application of command responsibility. Greater rank might confer greater authority, but with it comes the prerogative of holding someone else responsible when things go awry. On a day-to-day basis, a very senior commander is immediately responsible for almost nothing that occurs at lower echelons. There is always some subordinate available to take the fall.

As far as Bart Caldwell was concerned, responsibility for jeep accidents belonged to someone other than the Lord of the Ravens. None of his peers or superiors would disagree. By holding Sid Marks accountable for the unfortunate incident outside of Camp Rotz, he was adhering to standard practice. He was also putting himself in the clear.

Unfortunately for Caldwell, the CID investigation of that incident had introduced complications. Whether or not smuggling had played a direct role in this particular incident, the CID report indicated that it was commonplace along that particular stretch of the Czech border. An open secret among West German border agencies, the fact was not widely known among U.S. military authorities. Certainly, Caldwell had had no inkling of illegal cross-border activity in the regiment's assigned sector. But should the results of the CID's inquiry become known, that open secret could attract public attention. Caldwell would then likely find himself in very hot water.

After all, on his frequent heliborne tours, the RCO had assured everyone, from Big Al to Miss America, that the Ravens had eyes on the border.

Thanks to his ever-watchful regiment, the line that separated democratic West Germany from communist Czechoslovakia—the very frontier of freedom—was secure. That this was not actually the case would come as an unwelcome surprise to all those who had been told otherwise. Miss America would be disappointed, and Big Al discomfited; civilian authorities back in Washington would question the Army's basic competence; media outlets would have a field day.

Here, Caldwell recognized, was a problem of more pressing concern than a jeep accident resulting in two fatalities, or even the suicide of a troubled young troop commander. Neither of those threatened him personally. But any perception that the regiment's assigned sector was porous would be mortifying. To write off transborder smuggling— even of hymnals—as someone else's problem wouldn't cut it. Over and over, the Lord of the Ravens had portrayed himself as master guardian of the border. It was not a mantle that he could casually shed.

•

The day's big news back Stateside concerned a breakthrough in negotiating a new Soviet-American treaty limiting strategic arms. According to press reports, the agreement was, essentially, a done deal, assuming President Ford could persuade members of the Joint Chiefs of Staff and Defense Secretary Donald Rumsfeld to sign on. This, however, appeared to be a challenging proposition, one requiring Secretary of State Henry Kissinger to deploy all his formidable diplomatic skills.

For his part, Bart Caldwell devoted little attention to such lofty matters, whatever their relevance to basic national security. The centerpiece of his calendar for Wednesday was a daylong conference in Stuttgart. This quarterly gathering, nuclear disarmament initiatives absent from its agenda, brought together all the VII Corps commander's immediate subordinates. Substantively, the event served little purpose. Symbolically, it reminded the officers in charge of the various divisions, brigades, and lesser units scattered across the southern reaches of West Germany who they worked for. Those furthest from the flagpole, such as the 16th ACR, seemed sometimes to forget. Lieutenant General O'Malley used such occasions to exact renewed pledges of allegiance.

Before departing on the two-hour drive to corps headquarters—the weather was not flyable— Colonel Caldwell had summoned his adjutant to update him on the Sid Marks suicide. The prospect of cruising down the autobahn to Stuttgart was something to which the RCO was looking forward. In contrast, he was not in the least looking forward to delving further into the Marks affair. But there was no avoiding it.

When Tubby reported to the RCO's office, he found the Lord of the Ravens already at his desk. As ugly as it was imposing, the desk was itself a war trophy. According to regimental legend, just prior to

V-E Day, while sitting at this very piece of furniture, the last Wehrmacht commander of the kaeserne that now served as regimental headquarters had used his army-issue Walther P38 to blow his brains out. Whether true or not, the story linked the victorious Ravens of World War II with the vigilant Ravens of the Cold War, an uplifting narrative that excluded unseemly references to Vietnam. The 16th ACR was not alone in preferring this carefully curated version of the past.

Tubby disliked the legend and disliked the RCO's office, with its high ceiling and tall, narrow windows. Intended to overawe, the architecture always made Tubby feel like he should don a set of long underwear. It was cold as well as sterile. He also disliked the practice of exalting throne-like desks as symbols of authority.

As soon as Tubby entered, the RCO spoke.

"Tobias, what's the state of play regarding the L Troop matter? I'm leaving for Stuttgart in fifteen minutes. So, quickly, please."

Stifling a ripple of displeasure at the RCO's persistent presumption, Tubby summarized the essential facts: the events leading up to the Marks suicide; the absence of any concrete evidence regarding motive; the generally uninformative interviews with members of L Troop; his own visit with Emma; and L Troop's return to Pond Barracks, which was currently underway.

"You tasked the regimental chaplain to do something for the girl," he added. "Father Scanlan is working the problem, but with little to report so far. And, as you know, sir, there's a *New York Times* reporter nosing around. We can't say yet if there will be a story, or what slant he might take."

"That's it?"

Tubby's account had left out his meeting with Larry Kaplan.

"Basically, yes, except for two wild cards."

"And they are?"

"Race and Vietnam."

Caldwell scowled. Neither subject was a favorite of his.

"Explain."

"Had Captain Marks been white, his suicide would possess minimal newsworthiness. Instead, he was the regiment's only Black troop commander, who, prior to killing himself, was tagging the white officer who is currently his boss with criminal misconduct. No substantiation, but to a reporter, both are pure catnip. Take away those two factors, and no one would much care what happened on the border last week. Put them together, and the regiment has a problem. As do you, sir, in my opinion."

The RCO scowled again.

"Any recommendation?" he asked, making no mention of the CID report in his desk drawer.

"Talk to the reporter," Tubby said. "I don't know what advice you've gotten from your JAG. But as I see it, it's in the regiment's interests for this guy Kaplan—that's the reporter's name—to get his facts right."

"The coverup is always worse than the crime."

Caldwell was reciting the currently fashionable wisdom stemming from the Watergate scandal.

"Something like that," Tubby said. "The comparison is inexact, of course. In this instance, there's no coverup."

"No, of course not," Caldwell replied, shaking his head.

"And second-guessing whether Marks was suited for command is not much of a story," Tubby added. "Three shrinks will give you three different opinions. And if the *New York Times* wants to spend its money digging into events that Captain Marks claimed to have witnessed in Cambodia a half dozen years ago, let them have at it. Whatever happened or didn't happen back then has nothing to do with this regiment."

Tubby paused.

"Or with you."

"Okay, I hear you," the RCO said, glancing at his watch. "But right now, I need to run."

Tubby wondered whether the Lord of the Ravens had actually been listening.

Grabbing a thick binder of fact sheets containing various bits of trivia that the regimental staff had wasted days assembling, Caldwell stood and then hesitated for a moment, as if pondering a momentous decision.

"Set something up with this Kaplan guy," he said, "preferably for this evening, when I get back."

As he headed out the door toward the sanctuary of his waiting Mercedes, he snapped over his shoulder:

"And, Major, you had better be right about him."

●

By the time the Lord of the Ravens was pulling up to the entrance of VII Corps headquarters in Stuttgart, F.X. and Zaid were nearing the storefront in Nurnberg where Emma's mother worked and lived. The two-story building was located in a quiet neighborhood, blocks away from the bustling city center. Gold lettering on the large front window identified the owner: *R. Maier, Naherin*. Visible through the window were various garments, some hanging from racks or neatly folded on shelves awaiting pickup, others piled on a wide counter, with bits of paper attached. Behind the counter was a large clothespress of German manufacture. By all appearances, Frau Maier was a skilled seamstress with a loyal clientele.

A small brass bell attached to the doorframe announced the arrival of visitors. Seated behind a recent-model Bernina sewing machine, Renata Maier looked up and frowned. She recognized neither of the two men who entered, the one wearing the uniform of a U.S. Army officer, the other dark-skinned and shabbily dressed, with a beard that needed trimming. When F.X. introduced himself along with "my friend, Herr Muhammed," her frown deepened. She disliked men generally and harbored a particular dislike for men who were American soldiers or Black.

F.X. immediately sensed that this plain, unsmiling woman, her graying hair pulled back into a tight bun, did not welcome their visit. Irish charm was unlikely to win her over. So, he opted, instead, for directness.

"I come here seeking assistance, Frau Maier," he began. "Your daughter needs your help."

"I have no daughter, just as I have no husband," she replied, shooting Zaid a venomous look. "I am alone. And I much prefer it that way."

"Forgive me," the priest continued, "but you do have a daughter. As I believe you know, Emma is pregnant and will soon give birth. What you may not know is that the father of her child is dead. Captain Sydney Marks killed himself just last week. Emma has no one."

"How is this woman my problem? I warned her to have nothing to do with you Americans, with your money and your broken promises. I told her many times. She ignored me. Now, she must deal with the consequences."

F.X. nodded toward the crucifix that hung on the wall adjacent to the sewing table.

"I see that you are Christian. As a priest, I say this in all humility: Jesus teaches forgiveness. He calls on us to love one another."

Renate Maier shot out of her chair.

"I don't need an American to teach me about love," she said, visibly trembling. "Please, leave. At once."

The priest nodded, and without saying another word, he turned toward the door. Zaid, who had remained silent, now spoke:

"Your daughter has done nothing wrong."

"Get out!" Renate ordered, waving a large pair of shears at Zaid as he followed F.X. onto the sidewalk.

By the time the door had closed behind them, she had begun to sob.

Outside of Frau Maier's shop, the two men stood for a long moment. Neither spoke. Then, F.X. reached inside his field jacket and pulled out a half-empty pack of Marlboros. He gestured toward Zaid.

"Smoke?"

Zaid nodded and took one. The priest used his Zippo to light both cigarettes.

"I'm hungry," F.X. eventually said. "Let's get some lunch. Some place where we can talk."

"Follow me," Zaid replied, flipping his half-smoked cigarette into the gutter. "I know a quiet place not far from here. Favorite of mine. Cheap, too."

"Let's go."

The early afternoon sun was turning the previous day's snowfall into slush, which the priest in combat boots ignored. Wearing sneakers, Zaid did his best to dance around the piles of soggy muck, albeit with limited success. The day was warming, but his feet felt frozen. After walking several blocks, they arrived at a small Turkish café, which was packed and noisy.

"I thought we were going somewhere where we could talk?" F.X. asked.

"Well, most of these people probably don't speak English," Zaid replied sheepishly. "Besides, this place makes the best doner kebobs in the city. I'll order for both of us. You try to find a place to sit."

He vanished into the crowd, leaving F.X. to search for an empty table. Ten minutes later, he was back, carrying two doners, a can of Spezi, and a bottle of sparkling water. F.X. had failed to find an available table but was leaning against a counter with space just wide enough for them to share.

"Best I could do," he said, still slightly miffed at Zaid's misleading description of the café.

"You'll forgive me when you sink your teeth into the doner."

He was right. The doner kebob was delicious, and with a single bite, F.X. relaxed. Devouring the rest became the focus of his attention.

"How much do I owe you for this?" he asked, wiping his mouth with a paper napkin.

"Nothing. I'll get Kaplan to pick up the tab. He has a great expense account, and we're here doing background research."

"Excellent logic," F.X. said, noisily washing down the kabob with a mouthful of mineral water.

"If only this were beer," he added, belching none too quietly, "we'd be having a perfect repast. Now, speaking of research, what do you make of Frau Maier?"

"Well, she's bitter, and she's tough."

"With plenty to be bitter about."

"Your 'Jesus teaches' didn't help much. That's when she really erupted. It amazes me that people like you equate a display of symbols with actual faith. This is Germany, remember? There are churches on every block in every village, and crucifixes all over the place. Just as there were when Hitler ran the place."

"Sermon acknowledged, Zaid. So, we wasted our time?"

"Actually, I don't think so. You saw that Frau Meier was crying as we left. I think her tears spoke more loudly than her words. She still loves her daughter but can't bring herself to admit it."

"So, we do what?"

"Let's face it: You and I are among the few people on the planet who care about Emma. Your Colonel Caldwell goes through the motions but doesn't give a hoot about what actually happens to her or her baby. The U.S. Army has already washed its hands of this matter, just as it did back when Frau Meier herself was pregnant and alone."

"The world can be cruel."

"No shit. Take it from me: Any Black American can tell you what it's like to be regularly fucked over. Your golden-boy chum Hicks excepted, perhaps."

"Believe me, Major Hicks has his share of problems."

"I'd say he's someone who's had more than his fair share of breaks. The point is that Jesus and the Prophet, peace be upon him, are on the same page. So, you and I need to do what's right by Emma, even if it's just the two of us. I already have a wife and two kids, and I'm assuming you're not in the mood to get married. So that means we have to fix things up between Emma and her mom."

"And how do you propose we do that?"

"Wait for the baby. When she comes, she'll melt Oma's heart. We'll help arrange that."

"How do you know it will be a she?"

"Islamic intuition," he said dryly. "The point is I've got friends in Emma's neighborhood. They'll let me know when she goes into labor. They'll probably even take her to the hospital. So, when Emma delivers, we'll know, and we'll make sure Frau Meier does, as well. Then, we arrange for her to visit mother and child, and bingo, it's mission accomplished."

"You make it sound easy."

"It better be. Because after that, I'm out of ideas."

●

By the time the sedan carrying Bart Caldwell pulled into Merrell Barracks, the regular duty day had long since ended. Apart from the handful of soldiers pulling their shift in the ROC, most of the regimental staff had wisely left for the day. Tomorrow was sure to be busy, with the RCO doling out various taskings in response to the corps commander's pet concerns of the moment—a time-consuming drill with which all were familiar.

The office of the regimental adjutant was one of the few where the lights were still burning. At Tubby's invitation, Larry Kaplan had agreed to interview the Lord of the Ravens upon his return from Stuttgart. In the meantime, Tubby found himself keeping the journalist company. The two had swapped Vietnam stories—Kaplan had spent some time in Saigon when Tubby was at MACV headquarters, but they had apparently not crossed paths. As the afternoon dragged on, they had also done the crossword from that day's *International Herald Tribune* and consumed multiple cups of increasingly bitter coffee. Now, conversation was giving way to yawns. Both were gratified to hear the heavy door to the regimental headquarters swing open, announcing the RCO's return.

Lugging his briefcase, Caldwell walked wordlessly into his office. Tubby followed.

"Sir, Mr. Kaplan is here when you're ready."

"Okay, give me a minute then show him in. I'll want you here as a witness."

He ducked into the RCO's private lavatory. Tubby retrieved Larry Kaplan, sat him down at the conference table in front of the RCO's desk, and took the chair opposite.

Moments later, Caldwell returned, clutching a damp paper towel, which he threw into a waste basket. Without offering to shake hands, he planted himself at the head of the table. It had already been a long day, and he was not looking forward to being interrogated by some asshole reporter.

"What can I do for you, Mr.—ah—Kaplan?"

"Colonel, I was hoping we could discuss the circumstances surrounding the suicide of your L Troop commander."

As the reporter spoke, he flipped open a small notebook.

"What ground rules?" Caldwell asked. "On or off the record?"

"I prefer on the record. I'd like to be able to quote you."

"Okay, I've got nothing to hide."

Caldwell's tone conveyed more than a hint of wariness, as if suspecting an invisible trap just ahead. From his shirt pocket, he removed the torpedo-shaped Mount Blanc pen he favored for signing official documents. As both Tubby and Kaplan watched, he began doodling, making quick, random strokes on a notepad emblazoned with the regimental crest.

"So," he asked, "you think there's some sort of story there?"

Tubby sensed that he was watching a skilled predator silently stalking his unsuspecting prey. That he was unsure of who he was rooting for—the hunter or the hunted—made him slightly uncomfortable.

"Not so much in the suicide itself," Kaplan said, speaking without expression, "although that's certainly a tragedy. It's the larger circumstances that I find interesting. Background, context: that sort of stuff."

"I'm not following you."

"Well, let's start with Captain Marks. You have only a handful of Black officers in your regiment. Marks was one of those few. Did race play any role in your decision to assign him to command L Troop?"

"Obviously not. Command is a privilege. Captain Marks had earned his chance. Race had nothing to do with my decision. Frankly, the mere suggestion is insulting."

"Forgive me, Colonel, that was not my intention. But as his commander, surely, you knew that Captain Marks had experienced things in Vietnam that left him emotionally fragile."

"You're fishing, Mr. Kaplan," the Lord of the Ravens said, raising his voice ever so slightly. "War is a terrible business. But as far as I know, what

Captain Marks experienced did not differ appreciably from what hundreds of thousands of others did. Besides, the 16th ACR is a big outfit. Well over four thousand men wear this patch." He gestured toward his left shoulder. "I don't know—can't know—everything about everybody. I had no reason to suspect Captain Marks' stability, whether emotional or otherwise."

"Did you interview Marks before giving him L Troop?"

"No, I did not. After being posted to the regiment, Marks spent several months serving as a duty officer in the ROC. To be honest with you, now that we are out of Vietnam, the Army has more captains than it needs. Finding a suitable job for everyone can be a challenge. Putting Captain Marks in the ROC gave him a feel for the regiment. He did well there."

"Busy work?"

The RCO was now glaring at Larry Kaplan. He put down his pen.

"No. And any more impertinence, and we're done here."

"I'm sorry, Colonel. I'm just trying to understand why Captain Marks was given command of L Troop. I'm told there were plenty of other captains already waiting in line."

Tubby had been listening quietly but now spoke up.

"Mr. Kaplan, let me offer some of that context you are asking for. Part of my job is to maintain an order of merit list of captains eligible to command. Various criteria determine an officer's ranking on that list—time in grade, prior experience, performance within the regiment, and other factors."

"Including race?" Kaplan interrupted.

"Perhaps, but only as one consideration among several. Ultimately, what matters is the RCO's professional judgment."

"Of course."

Kaplan turned back toward Caldwell.

"Colonel, let me move on to a different subject, if I may."

Tubby felt a quiet sense of relief.

"Shoot," the RCO said, by now obviously irritated.

"The border. Your unit's primary mission, as I understand it, is to maintain active surveillance of the Czech border and to provide early warning of any incursion by Warsaw Pact forces."

"In our assigned sector, yes. Further north, a different regiment performs the same function."

"Are you satisfied with the resources that you've been provided with to perform that mission?"

"Well, I'd like to have some new equipment, especially helicopters, but basically, yes. The regiment is a very formidable organization."

"Yet, is it not the case that your regiment's actual presence on the border is very slight? A couple of aerial patrols and a handful of jeeps per day?"

Caldwell squirmed.

"We have other means of knowing what the other side is doing. Classified methods."

"So, the regiment's physical presence is mostly symbolic?"

"I wouldn't say that. Knowing that U.S. troops are present on the border reassures our German hosts, our NATO allies, and, above all, the American people. The border is secure because the U.S. Army is here—because my regiment is here."

"So, no one crosses without you knowing it?"

The RCO hesitated before answering, and Tubby held his breath.

"Here in our sector," the Lord of the Ravens said, "yes, that is correct."

Larry Kaplan finished writing then looked up.

"Thank you for your time, Colonel. I think that's all I need. Perhaps Major Hicks can show me out?"

The RCO nodded, clearly relieved to have finished the ordeal.

"Major Hicks, please do that, and then close things up here. It's been a long day, and I'm heading for my quarters."

"Will do, sir. Good night."

•

Bart Caldwell lived on a small semicircle of recently constructed homes reserved for senior military officers assigned in and around Nurnberg. Located not far from Merrell Barracks, it was a splash of American suburbia transplanted to Bavaria. The house came with the job. Large by German standards, it was not plush and was already beginning to show its age.

Although Harriet complained that their quarters were inadequate, given the entertaining expected of a regimental commander, she might have been howling at the moon for all the good it was going to do. This was what the Army provided to the officer commanding the 16th ACR, and it was a sight better than what many of Caldwell's peers enjoyed. He wished he could get his wife to understand that.

After entering through the front door and hanging his field jacket on the quartermaster-issue coatrack, he found her watching AFN in the small TV room adjacent to the kitchen. She glanced up, blew him an air kiss, and then returned her attention to an episode of *Kojak* that had run Stateside two years earlier. AFN broadcast in black-and-white on a single channel—take it or leave it.

"There's pork roast and mashed potatoes in the frig," she said. "You can warm them up."

Feeling more than slightly deflated, the Lord of the Ravens went to the refrigerator and grabbed a beer. He lifted the foil off the pork, took one look, and decided that it could wait. Bottle in hand, he wandered into the TV room and stood looking at his wife, trying to remember why they had first fallen in love. It all seemed so distant.

"Do you need something?" she asked, glancing up.

"I wonder if we could talk a bit."

"Uh, oh. What now, Mr. Serious?"

"I may be in trouble—potentially serious trouble."

Harriet clicked off the television.

"What have you done?"

"It's not anything I've done, but something I said."

"To whom?"

To avoid looking his wife in the eye, Caldwell took a swig of beer.

"To the *Times* reporter, Kaplan. He was waiting to ambush me when I got back from Stuttgart. Tubby Hicks had scheduled an interview."

"You're blaming your adjutant?"

"No, it was my decision."

"So, what's the problem?"

"Kaplan wanted to talk about the Sydney Marks suicide. I was prepared for that. But he also wanted to discuss the border, and that caught me by surprise."

"What did you say?"

"I told Kaplan that nobody crosses the border in our sector without the regiment knowing it. Which is what I have told countless others. And it's what everyone, from the corps commander up to Big Al Paterson and probably President Ford himself, believes to be true."

"It's not?"

The RCO shook his head.

"How long have you known this?" Harriet asked.

"Just a couple of days. The CID investigation of the Marks suicide found that the Czech border is a haven for smugglers smart enough to dodge our patrols."

"Smugglers! Smuggling what?"

"Cigarettes, booze, jewelry. All sorts of contraband. Even Bibles."

"Bibles? Whatever for?"

Harriet began laughing uncontrollably.

"Apparently," Caldwell said, "church groups back in the States are intent on converting the Godless communists."

"Poor Bart—undone by a bunch of Bible thumpers!"

"This is not funny."

Harriet struggled to regain her composure.

"Who has read the CID report?" she asked.

"Just me. It's locked up in my desk."

"And you propose to do what?"

"Hold the responsible officer accountable."

Caldwell was voicing a thought that had just popped into his head.

"But isn't that you?"

"Not really. Responsibility for the 3rd Squadron sector belongs to Hugh Massey. He's the one who has failed here."

"You're going to go after the Chief of Staff's son-in-law?"

"I happen to know that Big Al is not especially fond of Massey."

"And what will you do about the reporter?"

"I'll make sure that, in writing up his piece for the *Times*, he has his facts right. It's essential that he knows exactly who has failed here."

Suddenly feeling better, Bart Caldwell did an about-face and headed back into the kitchen to warm up his dinner.

•

While Tubby and Larry Kaplan had waited for the RCO, Zaid was onboard a plodding Bundesbahn commuter train headed toward Amberg. With most of L Troop now back from Camp Rotz, the *Times* reporter wanted Zaid to interview anyone who could shed light on the events leading up to the Sid Marks suicide. A couple of phone calls, and Zaid easily identified the gasthaus that was L Troop's favorite hangout.

By the time Zaid's train arrived at the Amberg bahnhof, it was pitch black, with the temperature dropping below freezing. The building itself was little more than a shed with a flat sloping roof and a total lack of adornment. As far as smalltown railway stations were concerned, the twelve years of the Thousand Year Reich had seemingly demolished any German taste for grandeur.

Zaid approached the stationmaster for directions to the Brauerei Bruckmuller, which turned out to be a considerable hike. Cursing under his breath that he was still wearing sneakers, he set out to find it.

The Bruckmuller was drab but obviously profitable. With badly scratched tables, chairs, and benches in need of replacement, and smudged gray walls badly in need of paint, it was, in American parlance, a bit of a dump. But in the middle of winter, the place offered warmth, along with good beer and decent food, plus a proprietor who didn't mind putting up with raucous G.I.s, as long as they had money to spend.

As Zaid took a seat at the bar, the place was just coming to life, the jukebox playing C.W. McCall's novelty hit "Convoy," which he found nearly unbearable. He asked the bartender for a mineral water and surveyed the swelling crowd of soldiers and young women, many obviously still in their teens. The scent of erotic possibility was palpable.

Hoping that it might serve as an icebreaker of sorts, he had donned his old OD field jacket with its frayed cuffs, the Ravens patch still visible on his left shoulder. However rancorous his departure from the Army, he had once, after all, been one of them, a fact that might prove useful.

A group of Black G.I.'s wearing jeans, Chuck Taylors, and bulky jackets swaggered in and commandeered a corner table. Zaid waited for them to order drinks and then ambled over.

"You guys in L Troop?"

"What's it to you, brother?" the tallest asked.

"Just asking. I'm a reporter doing some work for a Stateside newspaper. Hoping to get some background on Captain Sydney Marks."

He reached into his pocket and pulled out Larry Kaplan's card, embossed with the *Times* logo.

"Are you Kaplan? I know a few Kaplans back in Jersey City, and you don't look like one."

"No, my name is Muhammed, but I'm working on a story with Mr. Kaplan."

Zaid quickly shifted gears.

"What can you tell me about Marks?"

"Hardly knew 'im," the tall one said, the others nodding in agreement. "You gonna get me my name in the paper?"

"Depends what you've got for me. Was Marks a good CO?"

"Hard to say. He didn't do all that much. Top really runs things."

"Top?"

"The first sergeant. Chisholm. He's been in L Troop since, like, World War II."

"And he's good at his job?"

"Well, let's just say that he's good at taking care of things, starting with himself."

"I don't follow you."

"Look, Mr. Muhammed"—he put an exaggerated stress on the first syllable—"we see your Ravens patch and all, but we don't know who the hell you actually are, and we don't know what your game is."

"No game. Just looking for background. Sorry if I've stepped on any toes."

Again, he shifted gears.

"Were any of you guys on the mission to recover the remains of Sergeant Borski and Specialist Cotton?"

A short, heavyset soldier with a thin mustache spoke up.

"I was."

"See anything unusual?"

"Just Chisholm chewing on Wells and Hubbs. Whatever they did, it must have been big-time stupid."

"Wells and Hubbs were in the second jeep?"

"Yeah."

"I think you need to shut the fuck up, Williams," the tall one growled.

The table fell silent and stayed that way.

"Okay, sorry to have bothered you," Zaid said. "But before I shove off, are either Hubbs or Wells here?"

"That's Hubbs over there," Williams said, gesturing.

"I thought I told you to button it," the tall one said.

"Fuck you, Chico," Williams replied.

With a nod, Zaid stood up. He flipped them the peace sign, which drew a laugh.

"Duty, with Honor," he said with a grin as he walked away.

The tall soldier picked up Larry Kaplan's card and stuffed it into the pocket of his jeans. The others at the table turned back to their drinks.

Hubbs was sitting alone and was clearly well on his way to getting smashed. Without being invited, Zaid sat down and introduced himself.

"Who the hell are you, and what do you want?" Hubbs muttered, his speech slurred.

"Former Raven," Zaid answered, pointing to the patch on his jacket. "I used to be a scout in 1st Squadron, over at Bindlach."

"Which troop?"

"Cobra—C Troop."

"But you're out now?"

"Let's just say I was asked to leave."

"I wish they'd ask me to leave. Get out of this burg and back to Beantown. Sox. Celtics. You ever see Bill Russell play?"

"Can't say I ever did."

"I did, back when I was a kid. What a ballplayer."

Hubbs was fading fast. Without warning, he started singing "Dirty Water," beloved among Bostonians as a tribute to the city's notoriously polluted harbor. Midway through the second verse, he forgot the lyric and settled for humming the tune. Zaid saw his opening and took it.

"Mind if I ask you a question?"

"Not if you buy me another beer."

"Comin' up."

Zaid motioned to the bartender and held up a finger. The bartender nodded.

"I'm wondering why First Sergeant Chisholm was bawling out you and Wells when he got back from the crash site the other night."

"What's it to you?"

"Just say I'm curious. What had Wells and you done to piss him off?"

"Nuthin'. We'd done nuthin'. He just wanted to make sure we said nuthin'."

"About what?"

"Shhh," Hubbs said, his voice a hoarse whisper. "Keep your voice down." He glanced over at Chico's table. "I don't want those guys to hear."

"Said nothing about what?" Zaid asked, leaning toward Hubbs.

"About Top's little secret. His secret business."

Hubbs eyed Zaid's field jacket blearily.

"Hey, back in your day, did NCOs cash in on the side?"

"What do you mean cash in? How?"

"Kickbacks from the smuggling."

"What smuggling?"

"Across the border."

"No. At least, I don't think so."

"Well, Top's got it all figured out. He loves it when Lion pulls duty at Rotz. That's when he rakes in the dough. Wads of D-marks. I've seen 'em with my own eyes. How do you think he got that Rolex that's fancier than the RCO's?"

"What about the officers? Are they in on this?"

Hubbs laughed.

"Hell, no. Those morons are too stupid to know what's going on. Chisholm calls the shots. He gives a cut to some of the other NCOs then tells the rest of us to shut up or else."

He looked at Zaid as if seeing him for the first time.

"You wanna beer?" he asked.

"Not for me, thanks. But I've got one coming for you."

Zaid motioned again to the bartender.

"One more question: What happened on the night of the accident that killed Borski and Cotton?"

"Why should I tell you?"

"Because I'm buying the beer."

The answer appeared to satisfy Hubbs. He took a deep breath.

"Me and Wells were in the trail vehicle, me riding shotgun. It was fucking cold, so we just wanted to drive the route and get back to Rotz. Then, we came up behind a big white sedan, stopped in the middle of the trail. Three Krauts were pulling suitcases out of the trunk. As soon as they saw us, they threw the suitcases back into the trunk, got in the car, and drove off faster than hell."

"You followed them?"

"I don't know why, but Sergeant Borski started chasing them. Fucking stupid. No way we were going to catch up."

A thick-waisted woman wearing a dirty apron brought a beer, which Hubbs seized with both hands.

"What happened then?"

"What happened was Borski's vehicle hit some ice or something. It flipped and slid off the road and down the hill. Me and Wells could see right away that it was real bad."

"So, you did what?"

"Top had given us a radio freq to call him if anything went wrong. But I couldn't remember it, and neither could Wells. We figured Sergeant Borski had it. That's when we knew we were totally fucked."

He hesitated, as if lost in thought.

"Are you sure you don't want a beer?" he asked again.

"No, I'm good. But I need to catch a train."

Zaid stood up to leave, putting a few D-marks on the table.

"A train?" Hubbs asked, mystified. "Where to? It's fucking dark out there."

●

After showing Larry Kaplan out and extinguishing the lights in both the RCO's office and his own, Tubby had headed directly to his BOQ. He was not in the mood to go out for dinner, especially with a just-arrived letter from Isabelle in his pocket. He also needed time alone to reflect on the RCO's exchange with the reporter. It had been an unmitigated disaster.

Once in his room, he stripped, showered, pulled on jeans and a sweater, and put Coltrane on the turntable. He poured himself a generous ration of George D and slapped together a ham-and-cheese sandwich from fixings in his frig. If that didn't suffice, there were always canned sardines and crackers. Not for the first time, he reflected that life as a geographic bachelor had more than a few drawbacks.

Once settled, he propped up Isabelle's letter on his desk lamp, took a sip of whiskey, and tried to assess the implications of the RCO's blunders. The Lord of the Ravens had misspoken twice.

First, he falsely and needlessly asserted that race had nothing to do with giving Sid Marks L Troop. Given its ill-disguised enthusiasm for advancing the cause of racial equality, the *New York Times* was unlikely to raise a fuss if being Black played a role in Sid Marks getting a shot at command. That had been an unnecessary lie.

More seriously, Caldwell had stated categorically that nothing crossed the Czech border without his knowledge. Kaplan himself knew this to be untrue. If the RCO actually believed otherwise— if he was oblivious to illicit activity at a border that he claimed to have under surveillance—the paper would have a field day in pointing out yet another instance of military ineptitude. It would not be Caldwell alone or his regiment that would be embarrassed. The collateral damage would be extensive, with Big Al's "Good and Getting Better" mantra exposed as a sham.

How exactly was this Tubby's problem? Through some mysterious metamorphosis, probably traceable back to his cadet days, he had become deeply invested in the Army's wellbeing. He had no idea precisely how this had happened. But whether or not he willed it, soldiering had become akin to a calling. Now, here was Caldwell putting *his* Army at risk. Tubby deeply resented being implicated in a mess that his own boss had created. Even so, if anyone was going to undo that mess, or at least limit the damage, he himself would have to do it.

He finished most of his sandwich, looked at what remained with disgust, and threw it in the wastebasket next to his desk. Then, after a sip of whiskey, he opened Izzy's letter. It contained big news. She had turned down the job at UCLA and was about to accept a very attractive offer from Chicago. The miscarriage had shaped her decision. She wanted to return home. And she wanted to raise a family with Toby there, back where they had both grown up. What did he think?

On most nights, Tubby had little difficulty falling asleep. Not so on this night. The Sid Marks matter was about to blow up into something incalculably bigger than the suicide of a troubled young captain. And Isabelle's letter was nudging him to confront a question he had sought to defer or avoid altogether. Was it really *his* Army? Or was he meant for something else?

His mind spinning, he bounced back and forth between the two dilemmas, which became knotted together by the time he finally drifted off.

●

As Zaid's train pulled into Nurnberg's Hauptbahnhof, now restored to its prewar glory, he glanced up at the ornate station clock suspended from the ceiling. It was well past midnight. The various cafes and shops lining the walls of the station had long since closed. Despite napping on the train, Zaid felt exhausted. Reporting is damn hard work, he thought.

The bus that carried him back to his flat was nearly empty—just a couple of middle-aged Germans who eyed him with evident distrust. Men in the neighborhood with skin as dark as his were few in number. By the time he turned the key to his front door, his wife and kids had been in bed for some time. But before joining them, he called the front desk of the Méridien Grand and left a message for Larry Kaplan:

"We need to talk. I'll be in the hotel lobby at 8:30 this morning."

He hung up, fell into bed, and was instantly asleep.

●

Bart Caldwell also stayed up late, sitting alone, with the lights off, in the small TV room of his quarters. AFN had finished broadcasting for the night, so a test pattern showed on the screen. When Harriet had herself gone to bed, he had turned the volume all the way down, but left the set on. He, too, had poured himself a George D over ice.

After careful deliberation, he telephoned the ROC. Ezra Edwards, pulling the night shift, answered.

"Edwards, it's the RCO. Something I want you to do. Call the 3rd Squadron ops center and pass the word to Colonel Massey to expect me first thing tomorrow. Weather permitting, I'll fly to Amberg at first light."

"Yessir. Bindlach still on this morning, then Amberg first thing Friday. Is that correct?"

"Yes. Now get to it."

Caldwell hung up and went upstairs to bed. It was time for Hugh Massey to own his piece of the border.

IX

Thursday, 19 February

E zra Edwards did precisely as the RCO had directed, but he then took an additional step: He decided to notify Tubby. As the Merrell Barracks loudspeaker system finished playing reveille, he walked briskly over to the BOQ and rapped on the door of Tubby's room. He waited a few seconds then knocked again.

"Who is it?" came a groggy voice. "What do you want?"

Edwards identified himself. The door opened.

"Come in," Tubby said, dressed in plaid flannel pajama bottoms. He sat back down on the edge of his bed. "What's up, Ezra?"

"Sir, there's something going on that I think you need to know about."

"Okay, shoot."

Edwards described the RCO's late night call and plan to visit Amberg.

"So, why wake me up? The RCO is always going somewhere. It's part of his job."

"Sir, everybody knows about the newspaper reporter snooping around. And everybody's heard about some shenanigans on the 3rd Squadron border sector. I'm guessing that this is somehow connected."

"You guys in the ROC know too damn much," Tubby replied. But he smiled.

"Okay," he continued, "you done good. Give me fifteen minutes to shower and clean up, and I'll be in."

"Roger that, sir."

With that, Edwards left, pleased with himself.

Employing a skill that he and his classmates had mastered during their plebe summer, Tubby showered, shaved, and put on his uniform—buttons buttoned, seams aligned, boots shined—in a matter of minutes. By 0630, he had arrived in his office and was drinking coffee from a sturdy Ravens mug. He had grabbed a granola bar when leaving his room. This new-to-PX-shelves novelty would have to suffice for breakfast.

To catch the morning news, he tuned his portable radio to AFN. Then, he busied himself with paperwork while waiting for the RCO to appear. The headline of the day focused on Richard Nixon's upcoming trip to Beijing, where a warm welcome awaited the disgraced former president. Tubby had not yet fully processed what the changing U.S. relationship with the People's Republic signified. Apparently, some communists were bad while others were not, a radical departure from what he had been taught to believe back in Chicago.

The RCO arrived and went directly to his office. After a moment, Tubby followed.

"Sir, I understand you've added a visit to 3rd Squadron to your calendar. Bindlach for 1st Squadron training briefs today, then Amberg tomorrow morning."

"That's right, Major. 1st Squadron will take up all today, but then your classmate and I need to have a heart-to-heart. In the meantime, I want you to personally take care of something for me."

Caldwell reached into his desk and removed a manila envelope, which he handed to Tubby.

"Make a copy of this," he said. "Share the contents with absolutely no one—is that clear?"

"Yessir."

"Then, return it to my desk. Understood?"

"Yessir. Understood."

"Okay, let's hustle."

Caldwell glanced at his watch.

"I need to hit the road," he added.

The regimental photocopier—the only one in the building—was located in a windowless room down the hall from Tubby's office. A hand-written cardboard sign on the door declared: "AUTHORIZED PERSONNEL ONLY."

As soon as the RCO's bird lifted off for Bindlach, Tubby carried the manila envelope into the copying room, carefully opened it, and began feeding pages one at a time into the machine. The agonizingly slow process gave him ample opportunity to glean the essence of the document. It was the CID report regarding recent events involving L Troop. Within minutes, he realized that the contents were explosive.

Tubby now saw that the RCO's problem went far beyond a pair of soldier fatalities, or even an officer's suicide. And Caldwell had obviously decided to offload that problem onto Hugh Massey.

Tubby now realized, too, the implications of what the Lord of the Ravens had directed him to do. His compliance signified complicity.

Tubby had sworn fealty to the Constitution. He necessarily believed in press freedom. Yet, like most serving officers, he felt nothing but contempt for leakers. When Daniel Ellsberg, just five years earlier, had provided the *New York Times* and *Washington Post* with copies of the Pentagon Papers, he had embarrassed the entire national security apparatus, to include the leadership of the U.S. Army. In doing so, he had also violated a sacred trust.

Now, however, if on an infinitely smaller scale, Tubby was experiencing something of the anger that had motivated Ellsberg. More on impulse than after careful calculation, he reached the same decision that Ellsberg had.

Starting with page one, he made a second copy of the document for himself.

●

When Zaid showed up at the Méridien Grand, the lobby was bustling, but Larry Kaplan was nowhere to be found. He was, instead, camped in the spacious breakfast room, which is where Zaid spotted him, enjoying a soft-boiled egg with buttered toast.

"I have decided to go on a diet," the veteran reporter announced, "even though my resolve is suspect. But, please, join me, my friend. Help yourself to whatever you like."

"I'll take you up on that."

Zaid swerved toward the bountiful buffet table. By the time he returned with a heavily laden plate, Kaplan had finished his meal and was enjoying a cigarette, along with another cup of coffee. He poured one for Zaid.

"So," Kaplan began, "why the urgent summons to meet?"

"I took a train to Amberg late yesterday afternoon to visit L Troop's favorite off-duty hangout."

"And?"

"I talked to several G.I.s who confirmed NCO involvement in cross-border smuggling operations. It's a regular business."

"Who runs this business?"

"Chisholm—he's the ringleader."

"That's the first sergeant?"

"Yeah. But he's not the only one involved."

"Did you get names? Dates? Statements?"

"Uh, no. But I can connect you with soldiers who can. NCO involvement is an open secret. You need to make another trip to Amberg."

"Let me think about it."

"Okay. But while you're thinking, tell me this: How close are we to running a story?"

Larry smiled at the *we.*

"I've been in touch with New York," he replied. "My editor thinks there are loose ends that need tying up."

"Such as?"

"Number one, how much do Caldwell and Massey know about the smuggling, and how long have they known it. Number two, what are they doing to address the problem."

"So, you want to interview them both a second time?"

"Correct—Caldwell in particular. And I want you to get yourself back to Amberg pronto. This time, take a notebook, and bring back names, dates, and specific details. It's called reporting. And keep your receipts."

Zaid hung his head. It was a well-deserved ass-chewing.

●

As soon as Tubby finished making two copies of the CID report, he left the headquarters building and crossed the kaserne to the regimental chapel. The day was warmer than usual and the sky clear, about as mild a winter's day as Bavaria has to offer. He found F.X. behind his desk, smoking and reading one of Harry Kemelman's mysteries featuring Rabbi David Small. The priest had a well-developed taste for whodunits, especially when the sleuth was a fellow member of the clergy.

"Tobias Hicks in God's House," F.X. said, feigning surprise. "Has my good friend at long last found his Lord and Savior?"

"Not yet," Tubby replied with a grin. "But don't give up hope."

"Then, to what do I owe the honor of this visit?"

"Sydney Marks, I guess."

Tubby stopped smiling and took a seat facing the priest's cluttered desk.

"The case is about to break wide open, F.X. I could use some help."

"Bring me up to date."

Tubby summarized the contents of the CID report, concluding with the RCO's sudden decision to call on Hugh Massey.

"So, all of that means what, exactly?"

"Forgive me for being sacrilegious, but Amberg is fixing to be the site of a real come-to-Jesus meeting. Hugh Massey will learn that he is the RCO's chosen scapegoat. When Larry Kaplan drops his bombshell in the *Times,* Caldwell will be well clear of ground zero. Massey will be smack in the middle of the target area."

"How do you know that?"

"Because I've seen it often enough. Christ, so have you. Shit flows downhill. In Vietnam, it was an everyday occurrence. With Sid Marks dead, Hugh Massey sits at the bottom of this particular pile of shit."

"But why shouldn't he be held accountable? He's the 3rd Squadron commander, and that's where the security lapses occurred."

"Because, until about five minutes ago, the RCO proudly advertised himself as master of the entire regimental sector. God knows he bragged about it often enough in the aerial tours he takes such pleasure in conducting. Now, suddenly, he's tagging someone else as responsible for border security? Give me a break."

"And you aim to see justice done?"

"I'm just sick and tired of senior officers dumping on their subordinates."

"Plus, if I'm not mistaken, Massey is your friend and classmate."

"Classmate, yes. Friend, no. Hugh Massey and I parted company long ago."

"Okay, then, classmate. The point is that you're not a disinterested party. Anyway, what do you want from me?"

Tubby smiled.

"Well," he said, "right now, a smoke."

As Tubby reached for the open pack on F.X.'s desk, the priest tossed him his Zippo. Tubby fired up a Marlboro then slid the lighter back across the desk. F.X. picked it up and cradled it in his hands, as if it were a sacred talisman.

"Kaplan strikes me as a decent fellow," Tubby began.

"Whoa," F.X. interrupted. "Let me remind you that he's a reporter."

"Fair enough. But hear me out."

Tubby stared at the cigarette between his fingers then took a drag.

"He's also a combat veteran who fought in the big war and then covered our war. And he wants to see the Army find its way out of the fix it's in."

"How the hell do you know that?"

"He's said as much. Anyway, that's what my gut tells me."

"Even if that's true, so what?"

"So, when the *Times* runs Kaplan's story about soldiers in this regiment involved in border smuggling, it's going to be hugely damaging. I want to make sure the right people take the hit."

"And who might they be?"

"For starters, our regimental commander."

"Surely, you're not suggesting that the RCO is personally involved in criminal activity?"

"No, of course not. The chief crook is First Sergeant Chisholm, with other L Troop NCOs doing the dirty work. Kaplan will name those immediately involved—of that, I'm certain. But, as a good reporter, he's digging deeper."

Tubby reached for the porcelain Ravens ashtray on F.X.'s desk and extinguished his cigarette.

"Think about it: American soldiers profiting from smuggling through the Iron Curtain and getting away with it. How the heck does something like that happen? That's the question Kaplan will pose."

"The answer?"

"Dereliction of duty by the guy in charge. That happens to be our regimental commander—and nobody else. I aim to make sure that Kaplan arrives at that correct conclusion."

"How do you propose to do that, Tubby?"

"By asking for a huge favor. I want you to drive that creaky jalopy of yours to Amberg, where you will hand this to Hugh Massey. I'll let him know you're coming."

He passed the priest a thick envelope that had been taped shut.

"The CID report?" F.X. asked.

Tubby nodded.

"I've just made a copy."

"When do you want me to go?"

"This morning. Now, if possible."

F.X. glanced at his book and grimaced unhappily.

"In the meantime," Tubby continued, "I'll loan the original to Larry Kaplan. He'll read it, and I'll have it back in the RCO's desk by the time he returns from Bindlach."

Tubby paused and looked to his friend.

"What do you think?" he asked.

"I think that, by going after your boss, you'll be torching your own career."

"What career? I'm not exactly on the fast track to succeeding Big Al as Army Chief of Staff. Anyway, it's a risk I'm willing to take."

"Why exactly is this so important to you? I'm missing something."

"You know Big Al's marketing slogan: 'Good and Getting Better.' That's a crock. The Army is not good and getting better. It's broken. Our so-called volunteers are anything but the cream of American youth. Half of them probably shouldn't be in uniform."

"You paint with a broad brush."

"Maybe. But tell me I'm wrong. Vietnam gutted the NCO corps, leaving us with the likes of Chisholm and his cronies. Self-regarding pencil-pushers like Caldwell either don't see the problem or don't have the gumption to fix it."

"Okay, Tubby, let's say Caldwell goes. How do you know the next guy will be any better? He could be even worse. Have you thought of that?"

"I'm willing to take the chance."

For a long moment, F.X. said nothing, staring at the image of South Vietnam engraved on his battered lighter.

"Okay," he finally said. "I'm in. But you're not the only one whose butt is waving in the breeze. This isn't exactly like teaching Sunday School."

He picked up the manila envelope and used a slip of scrap paper to mark his place in the Kemelman whodunit.

"I'm off for Amberg. Dinner tonight at Ingrid's is on you, pal."

•

As F.X. set off for the 3rd Squadron headquarters, Harriet Caldwell was behind the wheel of her dark green BMW E21 sedan and headed toward Bamberg, home to 2nd Squadron. The car was a gift from her husband, purchased in gratitude for her loyalty and support as he had ascended the ladder to command the 16th ACR. Harriet felt that she had more than earned it.

For many years—no one could recall when the tradition had originated—the RCO's wife had from time to time informally gathered the wives of the three squadron commanders for a meal, gossip, and a chance to let their hair down, usually under the guise of cultural enrichment. The women had fallen into the habit of referring to themselves as the "Old Hens Club," though they were not old and would have taken umbrage had any of the regiment's younger wives called them hens. They did, however, rather enjoy their status atop the social pecking order that prevailed across the Kingdom of the Ravens.

Weeks before, Sally Wentworth, married to 2nd Squadron's Tommy Wentworth, had arranged for the Hens to tour Bamberg's famous 13th century Romanesque cathedral. Following the guided tour, they would lunch in a café and perhaps do a bit of shopping before going their separate ways.

This excellent plan had not taken into account the possibility of the L Troop commander committing suicide. Nonetheless, after only the briefest hesitation, all agreed on the need to carry on, despite the death of Sid Marks less than a week before.

Over the years, Harriet had visited a goodly number of European cathedrals. Even so, she was more than happy to add one more to the list. Besides, she enjoyed Sally Wentworth's company. Sally was stylish and full of fun. Harriet also felt an obligation to support Natalie O'Hara. Trapped in a bad marriage to 1st Squadron's Jim O'Hara, a notorious womanizer, Natalie had three kids under ten. Perpetually harried and usually late, she was sweet but not terribly bright. Worn down by her husband's infidelities, Nat always needed a morale boost. As for Connie Massey, while Harriet had never warmed to her, Bart had made it clear that she needed to get along with Big Al's only child. So, that was that.

Although the four women differed from one another in many respects, Harriet had come to see them as of a type. As Army wives, they had suppressed whatever anti-establishment inclinations they may have entertained back during their college days. They respected conventions. They conformed and coped. Expected to keep a positive attitude, they tried to oblige—even Natalie, to whom cheeriness did not come easily.

Each had chosen a husband. Their husbands had chosen the Army. The women were left to make the best of an imperfect deal. So, when their husband's assignment officer told him to move his family to some godforsaken post like Fort Polk, Louisiana, they did so, even if they might have preferred Fort Lewis in Washington or Schofield Barracks in Hawaii. They learned not to cause a fuss. Wherever they landed, solidarity with other Army wives of their generation was a primary value.

The women's movement had come too late for them. Had they been born even a half-generation later, things might have been different. It was all a matter of timing, and theirs had been unfortunate.

206 | Ravens on a Wire

There was no point in complaining. No one would have listened, least of all their husbands.

Harriet arrived in Bamberg with time to spare. She parked the BMW on a side street and walked to the cathedral. Sally was already there, along with their English-speaking guide, the vice-president of the local German-American Friendship Club. Tall, slender, and blonde, Sally was wearing her usual tight sweater and a very short skirt, a sartorial trademark that made her a great favorite among 2nd Squadron's young lieutenants.

Somewhat surprisingly, Natalie had also arrived on time. Neither tall nor slender nor blonde, she had succumbed to the early onset of middle age. Her personal trademark was a set of bulky plastic-framed eyeglasses, through which she eyed the world with a habitual squint. Her prescription was badly out of date.

After the ritual exchange of air kisses, Sally spoke.

"Ladies, as I was leaving the house, Connie called. She's running late, so I suggest we start and let her catch up."

The ensuing tour of the Bamberger Dom was Germanic in its thoroughness, with no architectural or historical detail overlooked. For American women possessing limited interest in medieval architecture, it was also tedious. Connie's eventual arrival a full half-hour late came as a welcome distraction. Looking a bit under the weather, she did not apologize for her tardiness. Her mind was obviously elsewhere.

"Ladies," Harriet said, "I wonder if this might not be the right moment to break for lunch."

This timely suggestion met with unanimous agreement. After thanking their guide, Sally led the group to her favorite nearby restaurant, the Edelfrei. Once they were seated, Harriet ordered a bottle of Sekt for the table then proposed a toast.

"Here's to Sally for hosting us for this enjoyable event."

The formal part of this very informal gathering thereby ended. The ensuing general conversation centered on their children's latest doings, events within their husbands' units, and plans for travel during the coming summer months. A second bottle of Sekt soon followed, with Connie opting instead for a vodka gimlet. All was light and innocuous until Natalie decided to introduce a new subject.

"Terrible what happened to Stan Marks."

"Sid Marks—his name was Sydney," Connie said, obviously irritated.

"Wasn't he Black?"

"Yes, he was Black. Why does that matter, Nat?"

"I just mean there are very few Black officers in the regiment."

"None at all in our squadron," Sally piped up.

Natalie O'Hara now had the bit between her teeth and was not letting go.

"Why did he kill himself?" she asked. "Any idea, Connie?"

"I hardly knew Captain Marks. He was new to the squadron."

"Something to do with Vietnam," Harriet said, hoping to steer the conversation in a less sensitive direction. "He was badly wounded and spent a long time recovering."

Connie said nothing.

"I heard that he got some German girl pregnant," Natalie said. "Is that true?"

"Yes," Connie replied between clenched teeth, "apparently."

"I feel sorry for her. Jim got me pregnant before we got married. That's a tough way to start off."

"Not a problem, in this case. There won't be a marriage."

"I know. I just meant…"

Natalie began twisting the fake pearls that hung around her neck. Harriet felt compelled to intervene.

"Bart has Chaplain Scanlan looking into what can be done to help the poor girl. In the meantime, can't we find something happier to talk about?"

Natalie either didn't hear or wasn't paying attention.

"Jim thinks that very few Blacks will make good officers," she said. "He'd never actually say that, of course."

"My father will tell you the Army won't get past Vietnam unless it recruits more Black officers," Connie replied.

"Well, if anyone would know, it's Big Al," Sally said, trying to be helpful.

"Sometimes, I think we'll never see the last of Vietnam," Natalie sighed. "We're just stuck with that awful war."

"What do you mean *we*?" Connie asked.

"I mean, it's like this dark cloud that hangs over everything."

"I don't think Hugh's hung up on Vietnam. He's moved on. So has 3rd Squadron."

"Oh, Connie, I wouldn't be so sure," Harriet warned.

Connie gave Harriet an angry look. After quickly draining the remainder of her drink, she pulled three 10 D-mark notes out of her purse.

"That should cover my share," she said as she stood up. "Ladies."

She nodded toward each, then unsteadily walked out.

"What got into her?" Natalie asked.

•

As soon as he returned from the chapel to his own office, Tubby asked the ROC to connect him with Hugh Massey. The word came back from Pond Barracks that the 3rd Squadron commander was not immediately available. He was teaching a class. Interrupt the class, Tubby ordered. Moments later, Massey was on the line.

"What do you want, Hicks? I'm busy. I'm discussing the warrior ethos with my lieutenants, as it happens. Not exactly up your alley."

"I've got something that requires your immediate attention, Colonel," Tubby replied evenly. "A courier is bringing you a report on the events leading to the Marks suicide. It's sensitive."

"Who is this courier?"

"Chaplain Scanlan."

"Your buddy."

"Perhaps, but right now, he's doing *you* a big favor. Just read the report."

Without saying another word, Tubby hung up. Moments later, Ezra Edwards appeared in the doorway.

"Sir, that Kaplan guy is on the phone. He's calling for the RCO. Do you want to talk to him?"

"Yes, Ezra, put him through."

The phone on Tubby's desk rang.

"Mr. Kaplan, Major Hicks here. You're just the person I'm looking for."

"How so, Major?"

"I have something you'll want to read. It's relevant to the story you've been working on. I wonder if I could bring it by."

"Absolutely. I'm in my suite at the Méridien. Room 732."

"I'll be there in twenty minutes."

Tubby hailed a cab outside the kaserne's front gate and made the trip in fifteen. Larry Kaplan had called room service to order a basket of pastries. As Tubby took a seat in the room, the reporter offered him coffee or hot tea.

"I'll try the coffee, please."

"So, what is it that I need to read?"

Without speaking, Tubby handed the reporter the CID report.

"I can't let you keep it," he said. "Take whatever notes you need, but the original leaves with me."

"How much time do I have?"

"I'll give you an hour. Then, I've got to get back."

Tubby picked up a croissant and, from where it sat on the breakfast table, a copy of that day's *International Herald Tribune*. He glanced at the front page.

"Nixon," he muttered with disgust.

Kaplan ignored him. With pencil and notebook in hand, the reporter was already hard at work.

●

Not long before noon, F.X.'s Opel wheezed up to the front gate at Pond Barracks. He flashed his ID to the gate guard, who saluted and waved him through. F.X. touched the brim of his cap in response and proceeded to the entrance of the squadron headquarters. By the time he turned off the ignition, Command Sergeant Major Moultrie had arrived to welcome him.

"Chaplain, if I may, you need to replace this heap with something more suited to your august position."

F.X. laughed.

"You've got that right, Johnny, but not just yet. Can I assume that you're here to take me to your boss?"

Moultrie nodded. F.X. got out of his car, and without bothering to lock it, he followed his escort into the building. They found Hugh Massey at his desk, pretending to work.

"Okay, Chaplain, what do you have for me? I've got a squadron to command."

"I have the CID's investigation into the Marks suicide. Your classmate made a copy of it for you — at great professional risk to himself, I might add. He asked me to deliver it."

F.X. dropped the envelope on the conference table, well out of Massey's reach.

"Mission accomplished," the 3rd Squadron commander replied. "Anything further?"

"None, Colonel. And no thanks expected. Just one word of advice: Treat the contents as close hold."

"When I need pastoral counselling, I'll be sure to call."

F.X. turned to Moultrie.

"I'll see myself out, Johnny."

Without another word, the chaplain headed back to his car, cursing under his breath.

The sergeant major waited until F.X. was out of earshot before speaking.

"If you don't mind my saying so, Colonel, you were a bit rough on the chaplain. We need as many friends up at regiment as we can get."

"Don't nag me, J.M.," Massey replied sharply.

"Yessir."

Moultrie saluted, turned about, and departed, stony-faced.

Once alone, Massey got up from his desk, sat down at the conference table, and tore open the CID report's envelope. Moments after he had begun reading, he realized the immensity of that favor. He felt a flash of embarrassment, which he quickly banished. Scanlan would get over any hurt feelings. Massey had more immediate concerns to attend to.

"Greta," he called out to his secretary, "fresh coffee, please. And make sure I'm left alone. No calls, no interruptions, unless it's my wife."

Then, he, too, like the *Times* reporter before him, picked up a pencil and notepad, and was soon writing furiously.

●

"Time's about up, Mr. Kaplan. I need to get back to the regiment before the RCO returns."

Larry straightened up and rubbed the back of his neck.

"Okay," he said. "I've got everything I need. I'm grateful to you for showing me this."

"Gratitude and fifty pfennigs will get me a hot cocoa," Tubby replied.

"True enough. But I now have answers to questions my editors have been pestering me about."

"So, when will the piece appear in print?"

"Don't know. The *Times* bureau in Washington will give the Army's PAO a heads-up and ask for comment. That might cause a delay. But my guess is this Saturday."

●

By midafternoon, per Larry Kaplan's instructions, Zaid had arrived back at Amberg via commuter rail. Without an ID, there was no chance of getting past the Pond Barracks gate guard, and it was too early for G.I.s in large numbers to congregate at the Bruckmuller. So, Zaid walked to the nearly empty gasthaus, took a seat, and ordered a coke. The jukebox was silent. But, perhaps, with a little patience, he would catch a lucky break.

He got the break, as it turned out, but not the luck.

As Zaid's soft drink was losing its fizz, Chico arrived, his retinue in tow. All four soldiers wore jeans, sweatshirts, army-issue combat boots, and ballcaps embroidered with NFL team logos. Chico claimed the corner table—his, apparently, by fiat—and ordered beer. Within moments, he spotted Zaid seated at the bar.

"Hey, Mr. Ay-rab, what are you doing back here where you don't belong?"

Zaid ignored the taunt.

"I'm talking to you, Moo-hamed."

Zaid pivoted on his stool.

"I was born in Georgia, you dumb shit," he said. "I'm as much of an American as you are."

"So, why you living in Germany?"

"Maybe, I like it here, asshole."

"You know, I gave Top that fancy card you were showing around. He says your kind ain't wanted in these parts. Why don't you just leave now and save us the trouble of kicking your fanny?"

"I'll leave when I want to."

"Nah, I think you'll leave right now."

Chico stood up, walked quickly over to the bar, and grabbed Zaid roughly by the arm. Zaid tried to push him away.

"Take it outside!" the barkeep yelled in practiced English, then, picking up a telephone, he calmly called the polizei.

Chico's companions dragged the squirming Zaid onto the sidewalk and held both his arms. Chico punched him twice squarely in the face, knocking him down. As Zaid struggled to get up on all fours, Chico kicked him viciously in the ribs then kicked him again. Zaid fell flat on the ground, moaning.

"This one's from Top, dickhead."

Chico again kicked Zaid, this time in the head.

"Now, take a hike, and don't come back."

With the distinctive singsong of a German police siren—"nee-nur, nee-nur"—now audible, the four soldiers walked unhurriedly in the opposite direction. They would escape to the relative sanctuary of Pond Barracks well before the two arriving police officers could apprehend them. Zaid's assailants could take their time.

Having broken up more than a few disturbances at the Bruckmuller, the cops were not notably sympathetic to Zaid's plight. This is what happened if you hung out in a G.I. watering hole. But they sat Zaid on the curb and checked to ensure that his injuries were not life-threatening and that no bones were broken. They gave him a bandage from their onboard first aid kit, which he pressed against his nose to staunch the bleeding.

Then, the cops drove him to police headquarters, where Zaid struggled to fill out a complaint destined to be filed and forgotten. The authorities in Amberg had more pressing matters to worry about than brawling Americans. Another short ride in a squad car deposited him back at the local bahnhof. How he would get from there back to Nurnberg was his problem.

●

Oblivious to the violence that soldiers under his command were perpetrating, Hugh Massey was still in his office, having read and digested the CID report. He had also spoken with a JAG officer he knew at corps headquarters. He had not consulted Pete Simmons, the regimental JAG, who reported directly to the RCO.

Since breakfast, Massey had had nothing to eat—just several cups of increasingly rancid coffee. He needed a break, and he needed something in his stomach. Although Greta had left for the day, Johnny Moultrie was still in his office, trying to talk a young M Company NCO into reenlisting.

"J.M., I'm heading to my quarters to grab dinner. Back in thirty minutes or so. If you're still around, I need to brief you on a sensitive matter."

Moultrie instantly sensed that something big was up. Except for Christmas Eve, the squadron commander never left the office this early. Neither did he, for that matter.

"I'll be here," he said. "Anything I can do in the meantime?"

"Yes, have Chisholm standing in front of my desk when I get back."

Although mystified, Moultrie nodded.

"Will do."

Massey grabbed his field jacket and headgear and was gone. As he stepped out into the late afternoon air, he took a deep breath to fill his lungs and clear his head. The biggest crisis of his tenure in command had just landed smack in his lap, but he found it strangely exhilarating. He felt energized, almost as if he were back in Vietnam, rolling out of basecamp at the start of an operation. By the time he slipped through the side gate and approached his quarters, he was whistling.

Instead of hanging up his jacket and hat, he threw them on a chair then went directly into the kitchen. Connie and the twins were already having dinner.

"Special deal tonight, girls. I need to talk to Mommy, so you two grab your plates and go watch TV."

His daughters did not object and quickly disappeared. Connie gave her husband a concerned look. He had neglected to give his wife a kiss.

"What's the problem, Hugh?" she asked as he washed his hands at the kitchen sink.

"It's the fallout from the Marks suicide. The CID's investigation has opened up a real can of worms. It fingers L Troop NCOs for being involved in illicit smuggling—looking the other way as Germans move contraband across the border."

"You're joking."

"I wish I were."

A saucepan of ravioli was warming on the stove. He helped himself to a serving and sat down. To forget the unpleasantness of her encounter with the

Old Hens, Connie had resumed drinking. Pausing now to freshen up her martini, she struggled to grasp the implications of this revelation.

"How long has this been going on?" she finally asked.

"For months—maybe years. Almost certainly before my time. That shit Chisholm is the ringleader and chief beneficiary."

"What are you going to do?"

"Read Chisholm his rights and place him under arrest. Then, J.M. and I are going to interrogate his partners in crime. I aim to flush out every shitbag involved, even if that means court martialing half of L Troop."

He was shoveling pasta into his mouth as fast as he could chew and swallow. The food seemed to fuel his anger.

"Vietnam poisoned everything," he said angrily. "Ridding the Army of those poisons is going to start right here right now."

"Shouldn't you notify Caldwell?"

"As it happens, the Lord of the Ravens is flying in here tomorrow morning. He already knows about the smuggling. He just doesn't know that I know."

Connie gasped.

"Should be an interesting meeting," he said with a mirthless smile.

Massey stood, noisily dropped his plate in the sink, and wiped his mouth with his hand. Then, he took a drink of water and kissed his wife on the cheek.

"Tell the girls I said good night."

As the front door closed, Connie got up from the table and topped off her drink, her mind whirling. Her first instinct in moments of crisis was always to consult her father. With Hugh not present to temper that instinct, she now picked up the house phone to place a call back to the States. This involved speaking with multiple operators, one of whom rang through to the spacious government quarters her parents occupied just outside of Washington.

An enlisted aide answered. Mrs. Paterson was out. That was fine, Connie said, since she wanted to speak directly to her father. He was in Texas, the aide replied, visiting Fort Hood. I really must speak with him, Connie insisted. Big Al had instructed members of his personal staff that, if his daughter needed to talk to him, they were to make it happen.

"I understand, ma'am," the aide said. "I'll track him down and have him call you right away."

Within ten minutes, the phone in the Massey quarters was ringing.

"Connie, it's Dad. What's up?"

By now, Connie had worked herself into a liquor-fueled state of weepy agitation. Not altogether coherently, she told her father that Hugh was in big trouble involving cross-border smuggling, with troops from 3rd Squadron implicated. Hugh, she said, was investigating, and Caldwell was set to show up at Pond Barracks first thing in the morning. After asking a few questions, Paterson pieced together the essentials of the situation.

"Okay, Connie, calm down. Let me look into this. Do not—let me emphasize, *do not*—tell either Hugh or Caldwell that we have spoken. Okay?"

"Okay, Daddy, I understand."

Shaking his head, Paterson hung up the phone. He turned to his aide-de-camp, patiently waiting nearby.

"Steve, call Stuttgart. I need to speak with General O'Malley. Now."

•

When Zaid's train pulled into Nurnberg's bustling hauptbanhof, he went directly to the nearest payphone and called the Méridien Grand. Larry Kaplan was in his room.

"I'm back from Amberg," he said, speaking slowly and with difficulty. "Some L Troop guys beat the crap out of me. Same ones I met the other night."

"Sonofabitch," Larry said indignantly. "Get a cab and come to the hotel. I'm in 732."

When Zaid arrived at the hotel's main entrance, he hastily crossed the lobby and took the first available elevator up to Larry's room. The door was slightly ajar. Wearing unpressed slacks and shirtsleeves, with a tie loosely knotted around his neck, Larry was on the phone, his tone heated. He took one look at Zaid, winced, and hung up. Although Zaid's nose had stopped bleeding, a dark bruise covered the left side of his face.

"You look awful."

"I feel awful," Zaid replied, trying to smile. "But I'll survive."

"Unfortunately, your night's not over yet, my friend. I want Hicks to see this. The so-called ROC says he's out, probably having dinner with Scanlan at the Goldener Fuss. Are you up for seeing them?"

"If you think it's a big deal."

"I do. When G.I.s beat up a reporter for doing his job, it's a very big deal."

Kaplan grabbed a scarf and overcoat, and they were out the door, headed to the elevator. When they exited into the lobby, Zaid's battered face and disheveled appearance caught the eye of several smartly dressed guests. It pleased him ever so slightly to be a source of their discomfort.

Cabs in Nurnberg were plentiful, and Larry had no trouble hailing one.

"Goldener Fuss," he told the driver.

Throughout the short ride, Kaplan said nothing. Zaid found comfort in the quiet. He closed his eyes and leaned back against the taxi's soft upholstery.

When they reached the gasthaus, Tubby and F.X. were already seated at their favorite table. Ingrid was hovering nearby, having just taken their order. The two men stood up as Kaplan and Zaid approached.

"Good God," F.X. muttered. "What happened?"

"Who did this to you?" Tubby asked, obviously shocked.

"Some of your own soldiers," Zaid replied between swollen lips.

"Good God," F.X. said again.

"Ingrid," Tubby said, "these gentlemen will be joining us. Please bring them something to drink."

Zaid took a seat at the table and asked for a cup of tea.

"Nothing for me," Kaplan said, still fuming.

"Now, tell us what happened," Tubby said, "in detail."

Zaid described the incident at the Bruckmuller, omitting only his own provocations.

"So, who exactly is Chico?" Tubby asked. "And why did he do this?"

"Identifying Chico should be easy enough," Kaplan interrupted, sarcastically. "Just ask L Troop's rogue first sergeant. More interesting is why Chisholm thinks he can get away with intimidating the *New York Times*."

"Look, Mr. Kaplan, what happened to Zaid is plain wrong. I get that. I'll call Hugh Massey tonight to make sure he appreciates the seriousness of this incident. You have my promise. And I'll brief Colonel Caldwell as soon as possible. Apart from that, what are you expecting from me?"

"I've learned not to expect much of anything from your regiment, Major. But I have enough regard for you personally to give you this heads-up: You already know that the story Zaid and I have been working on will soon go to press. As currently written, it will mean a black eye for your outfit, and a bigger one for the Army. When I add the detail of soldiers from your unit assaulting one of the two journalists covering the story, it will look that much worse. And now, if you will excuse us, I need to get Zaid home."

Without a further word, Kaplan left the table. Zaid trailed behind, his tea untouched.

Neither Tubby nor F.X. spoke. The priest looked forlornly at his half-finished beer.

"That's one way to spoil dinner," he said.

"Not a joking matter, my friend. The world's most influential newspaper is about to expose our storied regiment as a haven for crooks and thugs under the command of clueless officers."

"And this is your problem?"

"In a sense, yes. I mean, no: No one has put me in charge of anything. But, hell, it's a trainwreck. You tell me, F.X.: Am I just supposed to stand by and watch?"

"I don't know what you're supposed to do. But I think dinner just got put on ice."

•

When Hugh Massey returned from his quarters, Johnny Moultrie had First Sergeant Chisholm standing at parade rest in the squadron commander's office. With Massey's arrival, Chisholm snapped to attention.

Massey sat down at his desk and, without further ado, read Chisholm his rights and relieved him of his duties as first sergeant. He charged him with various offenses, to include conspiracy, larceny, and bribery. Asked if he wished to make a statement, Chisholm shook his head. Massey placed him under arrest, ordered him confined to his quarters, and directed him to speak to no one other than defense counsel.

"Sergeant Major, escort the prisoner to his quarters, and make sure that he stays there."

"You're gonna regret this, Colonel," Chisholm sneered. "You have no idea what you're doing. I know all about Bon Tri."

"We'll add disrespect to the charge sheet. Now, get him out of here, J.M."

As Johnny Moultrie marched Chisholm out, Captain Barney Doyle, the 3rd Squadron adjutant, peeked in. Recently promoted and new to his job, Doyle had just missed serving in Vietnam, reason enough for Hugh Massey to classify him as quasi-malingerer.

"Sir, apologies for interrupting, but regiment is on the line. Major Hicks wants to speak with you. He says it's important."

"No!" Massey roared. "I don't give a damn what Major Hicks wants. Tell him I'm busy. Now, get out of here, and send in those pathetic NCOs stacked up in the hallway. One at a time. Is that clear?"

"Yessir. Very clear."

Like a spanked puppy, Doyle slunk back to his own desk.

Getting Chisholm's accomplices to own up to their roles in the smuggling racket turned out to be a simple matter. With their ringleader facing the prospect of a general court martial, all but two caved, in effect begging for mercy. From each, Massey demanded a written admission of guilt. The two holdouts sat in Johnny Moultrie's office, contemplating the prospect of pretrial confinement in the Army's Mannheim jail.

It was nearly midnight by the time Massey wrapped up his interrogations. Feeling both exhausted and energized, he summoned his sergeant major into his office.

"Let's call it a day, J.M."

"Yessir, and a long one. But about Bon Tri…"

"What about it?"

In an instant, Massey's tone had become chilly.

"Look, sir, every NCO in the squadron— probably in the whole regiment—knows that something happened there during Cambodia. And that you were involved—somehow."

"What does every NCO supposedly know?"

"That there was an incident in some little ville, involving troops you were commanding."

"What sort of incident?"

"A massacre of Cambodian civilians."

Moultrie sounded apologetic.

"You believe that?" Massey asked.

"No, I wasn't there. But you know how the rumor mill works. Once a story gets around, it doesn't go away."

"Well, put your mind at rest, J.M. I was not involved in killing civilians at Bon Tri or anywhere else."

"Yessir, understood. But when Chisholm goes to trial, he'll try to discredit his accuser. That's you."

"Let him. He's a liar, a cheat, and a thief with zero credibility. Now, let's get out of here."

As he turned out the lights in his office, Massey noticed his adjutant still at his desk.

"Why are you here, Bruno?" Massey found it inexplicably entertaining to mangle Captain Doyle's first name.

"Sir, Major Hicks told me you need to call him tonight, no matter how late."

"Dammit. Okay, get him on the line. But make it snappy. I want to get out of here."

The phone rang on Massey's desk.

"What do you want, Hicks? I'm tired."

Tubby suppressed the impulse to say that, having waited several hours for Massey's call, he, too, was tired.

"Two things you need to know, Colonel. First, the *Times* exposé is set to run. It's now Friday morning Stateside. The piece will appear on Saturday, with early editions out the evening prior, probably a dozen hours from now. That's when the shit will really hit the fan."

"Got it. What's the second thing?"

"The *Times* report will include a specific detail that you won't like. Several hours ago, several goons from L troop beat the crap out of the *Times* stringer who was researching the article. The impression is that they did so at Chisholm's behest. The further impression is that you're not in control of your own unit."

"Why wasn't I told about this?"

"Because you refused to take my call this afternoon."

X

Friday, 20 February

The Lord of the Ravens had returned from Bindlach late Thursday evening. As expected, the 1st Squadron training briefing had consumed the entire day. Caldwell typically found great satisfaction in this quarterly ritual, with its endless array of charts purporting to depict what the squadron had recently accomplished and what it would do in the months ahead.

In truth, the correlation between charts and reality tended to be sketchy. But, by unspoken agreement, Caldwell and his subordinates pretended otherwise, thereby allowing the RCO to question, probe, and pontificate about what to improve or do differently. Within forty-eight hours, all parties concerned would have forgotten the entire exercise. But the event itself captured the essence of Caldwell's philosophy of command: Substance took a backseat to appearance. Jim

O'Hara, commanding 1st Squadron, knew the drill and had played along. It was, in Army slang, a dog-and-pony-show.

On this occasion, however, Caldwell's coming showdown with Hugh Massey cast a pall over the occasion. The RCO was unusually grumpy, leaving the bewildered O'Hara to wonder if he had somehow misread the boss' signals. Given the paramount importance attributed to keeping the RCO happy, O'Hara would have eagerly apologized, if only he knew where he had gone wrong.

A poor night's sleep did not improve Caldwell's mood by Friday morning. He had gone into the office exceptionally early. Once at his desk, he silently rehearsed how he would present Hugh Massey with a copy of the CID report and, citing his failure to maintain border security, relieve him of his post. An ugly scene would surely ensue. He would need to exhibit self-control. Massey would blow up, thereby further demonstrating his unfitness for command.

A knock on the door interrupted his train of thought. It was his adjutant.

"Sir, regarding that document you gave me yesterday: Both the original and one copy are in your desk."

Caldwell nodded. "Yes. I have them."

"But before you leave for Amberg," Tubby continued, "I need to update you on two things."

"Okay, Major, shoot."

Tubby sensed that Caldwell's mind was elsewhere. Even so, he repeated what he had told

Hugh Massey. That the *Times* story would break in a matter of hours seemed not to register. Instead, Caldwell latched onto the assault of Zaid Muhammed, which he treated as further evidence of Massey's failure as a commander.

Tubby made one last effort to get the RCO's attention.

"Colonel, I don't pretend to know exactly what sort of reaction the *Times* story will unleash. I can tell you that, when I was at MACV in 1970, the press response to Cambodia was fierce. We need to brace ourselves for a media storm, both American and German. Network TV, too. And we need to have a response ready."

"You handle it," the Lord of the Ravens replied. "I have more immediate issues to attend to."

●

Whenever Quickdraw 6 flew into Amberg, his bird put down at the airstrip just above Pond Barracks. Used during World War II for small single-engine Luftwaffe aircraft, it had since become home to the local glider club. Of the original airfield, little remained, apart from a torn windsock and a dilapidated hangar missing its doors and badly in need of a new roof.

As the Lord of the Ravens dismounted from his Huey, Johnny Moultrie was waiting alongside the squadron commander's sedan to drive him to the squadron headquarters. The ground was still soft from the recent thaw, and muck caked Moultrie's boots. That Hugh Massey had sent his sergeant major to greet the RCO rather than coming himself was a none-too-subtle slight.

Caldwell ignored the sedan and began walking toward the kaserne, visible in the near distance.

"Let's hoof it, Johnny. I could use some exercise."

Never quite having accustomed himself to officers' propensity for pettiness, Moultrie fell in step alongside.

"A great day to be a soldier," he observed, the cliché seeming like a safe conversational gambit.

"Indeed," the RCO replied, obviously not in the mood to chat.

For the remainder of the brief walk, neither man spoke.

Unused to seeing such an exalted presence striding through their midst at the start of a duty day, members of 3rd Squadron either saluted and shouted "Duty, with Honor, Sir," or froze in their tracks until the Lord of the Ravens passed by.

When Moultrie escorted Caldwell into the headquarters building, both men leaving a trail of mud behind them, they went directly to the squadron commander's office. They found Hugh Massey seated behind his desk with his hands folded. As the RCO entered, Massey stood, albeit without making any pretense of assuming a position of attention. Moultrie silently wondered if the shenanigans would ever end.

"J.M., please close the door when you leave," Massey said before turning to the RCO. "Sir, you wanted to see me."

The two men faced each other across the width of the squadron commander's desk, their mutual hatred on full display.

"Lieutenant Colonel Massey, I am suspending you from your position as 3rd Squadron commander, effective immediately. I expect by day's end that the corps commander will confirm your relief."

"On what basis?" Massey asked, his voice dripping with scorn.

"Dereliction of duty. Your squadron is charged with securing a portion of the Czech border. You have manifestly failed to fulfill that responsibility."

"Based on what evidence?"

"Based on a comprehensive investigation."

Caldwell dropped the CID report on Massey's desk.

"It found," he continued, "that senior NCOs under your command have engaged in massive transborder smuggling. This alone is evidence of gross negligence on your part."

"I've seen that CID report," Massey said, the revelation catching the RCO by surprise. "And if I'm guilty of negligence, I'm not alone. The buck doesn't stop in Amberg. You own a piece of this."

"How did you get that document?"

In an instant, Caldwell knew the answer to his question.

"A friend," Massey jeered. "I read it just yesterday, and since then, I've busted the crooks involved. Problem solved."

"Too little, too late," Caldwell replied.

"We'll see about that. You're about to become front page news back in the States, Colonel. Good luck trying to explain the crime wave that happened right under your nose."

"I'll take my chances. Good luck explaining how your soldiers beat up a *Times* reporter yesterday."

Despite his intentions, Caldwell's voice had risen.

"I'll nail them, too," Massey said.

"Too little, too late," Caldwell repeated. "Face it, Massey, you're through. You are an embarrassment to the regiment. I suggest that you clean out your desk and tell that alcoholic wife of yours to start packing."

None too happy with the way the interview had unfolded—he had not meant to lose his cool—Caldwell glanced at his Rolex then turned to leave. Moultrie was patiently waiting outside the door, having listened in amazement to the entire exchange.

"Sergeant Major, tell my bird to crank. I'm returning to Nurnberg."

Waving off the offer of a ride to the airfield, the RCO headed back to his waiting helicopter on foot, Moultrie following at respectful distance. By the time they arrived, several inches of mud caked the soles of their boots. As Caldwell mounted the chopper, the sergeant major saluted.

"Duty, with Honor, sir."

•

Following his suspension from command, Massey had remained standing. Now, in a blind fury, he grabbed the Ravens coffee mug on his desk and flung it at the far wall, knocking to the floor a framed photo of his most recent promotion ceremony. When the glass shattered, he let loose a string of profanities.

"Greta," he bellowed. "I'm going to my quarters."

Slamming the door to his office, Massey bulled his way out of the building, hatless, jacketless, and oblivious to the look of wonder on Barney Doyle's face as his squadron commander charged by. It was as if one of the gods was melting down in plain sight.

Having packed the girls off to school, Connie was home alone, nursing a coffee and a hangover. As the front door slammed, she jumped. One glance at the look on her husband's face, contorted with rage, and she knew something terrible had happened. She said nothing while Massey paced back and forth the length of the kitchen. Only after a long minute could he bring himself to speak.

"That worthless prick thinks he's going to fire me, Con. Well, fuck him. We'll see who's going to take the fall. And it's not going to be me."

He leaned against a kitchen chair to steady himself. Gradually, his breathing returned to something like normal, and he recounted his confrontation with Caldwell. Her reaction was predictable.

"I'll call Dad."

"No, you won't. I forbid it. Involving your father will only make matters worse."

"Then, what, Hugh?"

Massey was still struggling to collect himself.

"Call my ex-buddy Tubby Hicks," he finally said. "Hicks is tight with that reporter, Kaplan. We need the *Times* story to point the finger at Caldwell. Hicks might be able to help. Tubby has always liked you, Con. Talk to him. See what he'll do for us."

Connie suddenly felt compromised, as if nudged toward something sleazy. But she saw no alternative to doing as her husband asked. Their partnership required as much. As Massey stalked back to his office, slamming the front door of their quarters behind him, she picked up the house phone and asked the operator to connect her with the ROC. Was Major Hicks available? Within a minute, he was on the line.

"Connie, what can I do for you?" he asked, knowing instinctively that this was a conversation he didn't want to have.

"Tubby, Caldwell just left here. He relieved Hugh—fired him. This is so unfair. We don't know where to turn. What should we do?"

Connie had begun to cry.

"I'm not sure I can do anything, Con," Tubby said, wondering at the assumption that Massey's problems were necessarily his.

"Can't Kaplan put Hugh in the clear?"

"The piece is written, Connie. It will be on New York newsstands within hours. The priority is now damage control."

"Well, what can you do to protect Hugh?"

"I don't know. Hugh isn't the only one at risk. So is Caldwell and the regiment. So is the whole Army, which is about to get a huge black eye."

"I don't care about Caldwell or his regiment or the Army."

"I understand, Con, but I don't have that luxury."

"So, you won't help us."

In an instant, her appeal for help had become an indictment. Tubby stood charged with betrayal.

"Easy, Con. I'll talk to Kaplan. But don't expect any magic. He's not my friend. Reporters don't have friends. Or at least they shouldn't."

Clearly disappointed, Connie Massey hung up. Tubby briefly wondered what she had actually heard and what she would pass along to her husband. A knock on the door interrupted his reverie. It was Ezra Edwards, a sly grin on his face.

"Boss, that guy Kaplan is on the phone. Do you want to talk to him?"

Tubby nodded. To clear his head, he followed Edwards down to the ROC and took the call there.

"Mr. Kaplan. Just the person I was hoping to speak with."

"Likewise, Major. I wonder if we could meet—today, if possible. I think it would be mutually beneficial."

"When and where? I'm at your disposal."

"Let me propose this: I'll get a cab and pick you up at Merrell Barracks in twenty minutes. I want to look in on my friend Zaid to make sure he's okay. We can talk on the way."

"And I can reiterate the regiment's apologies for what happened yesterday in Amberg."

"As I was hoping you would. I'll see you in twenty minutes, then."

●

Upon his return from Amberg, the Lord of the Ravens had gone directly to his quarters. He told the ROC that he would report back to the regimental headquarters later, without specifying a time. Events were not unfolding as he had intended. Caldwell had always prided himself on his ability to anticipate surprises and to plan accordingly. Now, he desperately needed to formulate a new plan.

Tubby's immediate priority, meanwhile, was to keep word of Massey's relief under wraps for as long as possible. Considered from that perspective, the RCO's momentary absence was fortuitous. Grabbing his ballcap and field jacket, Tubby slipped out of his office, telling no one where he was going. At the entrance to the kaserne, a cab was idling. Larry Kaplan rolled down a window and told him to get in.

As soon as Tubby had settled in the backseat, Kaplan handed him a sheaf of paper.

"What's this?" Tubby asked.

"A fax of what will appear on tomorrow's front page. Read it."

Tubby did as instructed. The article was detailed, devastating, and accurately reported, with an overarching theme of U.S. military malfeasance, criminality, and senior officer cluelessness. Barton Caldwell and Hugh Massey figured prominently and unfavorably. The tragedy of Sydney Marks qualified for only passing mention. By the time the taxi arrived at Zaid's apartment block, Tubby had digested the contents.

"A very fine piece of journalism, I'm sorry to say. But why have me read it now, before it's published?"

"Because this won't be a one-day story. My editors will expect follow-up. They'll want me to dig deeper. What breaks tomorrow will only be round one."

"And you're expecting my help with round two? If so, you're in for a disappointment."

"No, I respect you too much even to suggest such a thing. What I'm expecting—or hoping for—is mutual accommodation."

They had exited the cab and were approaching the entrance of Zaid's building. Here, they stopped.

"I don't understand what you're getting at," Tubby said.

"Let me spell it out. My interest—and my paper's interest—is to understand how something like this could happen. How could the U.S. Army have once more fallen down on the job so badly? What does this failure tell us about the Army's efforts to recover from Vietnam? That's the bigger story here."

"Okay, I get that."

"Your interest, if my guess is right, is to protect your regiment's reputation and to deflect public perceptions that the Army, as a whole, is still on its ass."

"Fair enough."

"Where your interests and mine overlap, then, is on the issue of accountability. Who should be held responsible for the lapses in border security that the *Times* is about to expose? Who fucked up? First Sergeant Chisholm? Big Al Paterson? Or people in between? What's *your* answer to that question, Major?"

Tubby did not answer immediately. After a long pause, he responded with a question of his own.

"Why not ask the RCO or Hugh Massey? Why is my opinion so important?"

"Because, as far as I can tell, you're the only one in this sordid story who possesses some sort of moral compass. In my opinion, your judgment carries weight."

Once again, Tubby fell silent. Kaplan waited.

"Okay, take out your notebook," Tubby said. "Here's what I think: In this regiment, the principle of command responsibility is inviolate. It will remain so."

"Which means what?"

"It means that commanders at all levels are responsible for what their unit does or fails to do. No excuses, no exceptions."

"I can quote you?"

Again, Tubby hesitated.

"Yes," he finally said.

Larry flipped his notebook shut.

"Okay, got it. Let's check in on Zaid."

As Kaplan was reaching for the bell, the door to the apartment swung open. It was Zaid.

"I saw the two of you jawing through the window. Didn't want to interrupt. Please, come in."

As they entered, they glimpsed a woman dressed in an ankle-length skirt, long-sleeved tunic, and headscarf ducking into a back room, a squalling youngster under each arm.

"Wife and kids," Zaid said apologetically. "The place is a bit untidy, I'm afraid. But toss those toys on the floor and find a place to sit. Can I get you something? Tea, perhaps? Juice?"

Tubby and Kaplan declined the offer and remained standing.

"Zaid, we apologize for barging in like this. Major Hicks and I just want to see how you're doing."

"And to offer my personal assurance that your attackers will get what they deserve," Tubby interjected.

"Thank you—both of you—but I'm doing okay," Zaid said with a crooked smile. "Just make sure Chico gets his ass kicked."

"Well, we don't want to keep you from your family," Kaplan said. "But let me leave you with this."

He handed Zaid the fax that Tubby had read.

"It's the piece that your reporting made possible. I won't forget your contribution. Nor will the *Times.* You can expect generous payment."

"It's out when?"

"Tomorrow morning, New York time."

Zaid grinned, obviously pleased. He was still grinning as Tubby and Kaplan let themselves out.

"One more thing," he shouted from the doorway as they walked back to their waiting taxi. "Emma is in the hospital! She's having her baby!"

•

In more than a decade of commissioned service, Tubby had never consciously shirked his duty. Now, however, as Larry Kaplan dropped him off at the front gate of Merrell Barracks, he found the prospect of returning to his office too much to bear.

Instead, he skirted past the regimental headquarters to the post gym, all but empty during duty hours. A bored young soldier oversaw the premises. He handed out towels, kept an eye on equipment, and made sure the building didn't burn down.

Tubby wandered onto the court and scooped up a loose ball.

"You're not supposed to wear boots on the gym floor," the attendant said uncertainly.

Tubby ignored him, and the attendant chose not to press the point.

Dribbling onto the court, Tubby began shooting baskets from the top of the key. He had not lost his touch.

The feel of the ball rolling off his fingertips ignited old feelings of hope, possibility, and innocence—the great qualities of youth now largely spent with the onset of middle age. Going back to his boyhood days in Chicago, shooting hoops was the closest Tubby came to a religious experience. He knew he would miss it dearly when his playing days ended.

Early editions of tomorrow's *New York Times* would go on sale well after nightfall in West Germany. That's when all hell would break loose. Larry Kaplan had warned Tubby to expect inquiries from other major American papers and the three commercial TV networks, just for starters. Lapses in border security would prompt questions from German and British media. The London tabloids would jump all over the story. *Stars & Stripes* would expect a detailed explanation. Of more pressing concern, so, too, would the White House and Congress.

By the time he finished his impromptu workout, Tubby was covered with sweat. Changing into a fresh uniform would further delay his return to work—an appealing prospect. So, when he left the gym, he swung by his BOQ. There, he found a cigar taped to his door, along with a 3 x 5 card bearing F.X.'s nearly illegible scrawl.

"Congratulations!" it read. "It's a girl!"

So, Emma had delivered. On the reverse side of the card was a note: F.X. and Zaid intended to check on Emma that afternoon. He planned to have dinner at Ingrid's afterwards and hoped to see Tubby there.

Not this time, Tubby thought.

When Tubby got back to the regimental headquarters, the RCO had already returned from his quarters. He had closeted himself in his office, constantly on the phone. When Tubby tried to brief him on the coming media storm, Caldwell refused to be interrupted. He obviously had other things on his mind.

Ezra Edwards solved the mystery. The ROC had received a TWX from VII Corps Headquarters announcing that Lieutenant General O'Malley's fixed-wing would arrive at Feucht Army Airfield outside of Nurnberg at 1600 hours that afternoon. The message provided further detail that was as ominous as it was cryptic. The corps commander wanted the RCO waiting for him outside of the airfield's small VIP lounge. Their meeting would take no more than 10 minutes, at which time Colonel Caldwell would be free to depart. O'Malley would remain for a separate meeting with an unspecified individual.

Beside himself with curiosity, Sergeant Edwards duly passed along these instructions to Tubby. After quickly reading them, Tubby knocked on the door to the RCO's office and entered without being invited. He placed the TWX directly in front of Caldwell, who read it and waved his hand as if to dismiss both message and messenger. He then resumed speaking on the telephone. Tubby shrugged and returned to his own office.

As he sat down at his desk, his phone rang. It was O'Malley's aide, calling from Stuttgart to inform him that he was the unspecified individual mentioned in the TWX. When the General had finished with Caldwell, he wanted to see Tubby, who was to present himself at the VIP lounge at 1615. This, too, would require no more than a few minutes. The corps commander had a social engagement later that day and could not afford to be late.

Tubby immediately returned to the ROC and pulled aside Sergeant Edwards.

"Ezra, I'm going to need a ride to Feucht. Is the duty driver available to give me a lift?"

"Colonel Caldwell is just about to depart for that location in his limo," a brash young PFC named Houlihan volunteered. "Couldn't the Major just tag along with the RCO?"

"Absolutely not," Edwards interjected, treating Houlihan to a withering look. "Major Hicks, the ROC will get you there and anywhere else you need to go."

Steamed at Houlihan for his temerity, Edwards ordered him to drive Tubby. As a recent arrival, the young soldier hadn't the faintest idea how to get to Feucht.

"No problem," Tubby said as he climbed into the front seat of an OD Green sedan. "Follow my directions."

He wondered if Houlihan was even licensed to drive, but after brief reflection, he thought it better not to ask.

●

When the Lord of the Ravens arrived at Feucht, the corps commander's plane had entered the landing pattern. As it settled onto the runway and rolled to a stop, the RCO left his Mercedes and approached. A short distance from the aircraft, he halted and stood at attention, allowing General O'Malley to deplane.

Followed by his aide, O'Malley exited the aircraft. Once on the tarmac, he motioned toward Caldwell and began walking directly toward the VIP lounge. Although he had returned the RCO's salute, he did not offer to shake his hand. Caldwell fell in mutely behind.

The lounge had a look of semi-abandonment, with cracked floor tiles, broken blinds covering filthy windows, and an array of mismatched metal furniture. A wastebasket overflowed with trash. The sole amenity was a watercooler that didn't work. O'Malley made a mental note to call the airfield commander, who was obviously in need of some serious counselling.

"Okay, Quickdraw, please sit down. This will not be pleasant for either of us."

After removing their ballcaps, they settled into chairs facing each other across a small table. O'Malley took a deep breath, exhaled, and sighed.

"I'm relieving you from command, Colonel, effective immediately. Your regiment has failed in its assigned mission of border security. With that failure about to become public, the entire Army will suffer enormous embarrassment. You're a fine guy, Bart, but this smuggling business involving your own troops is totally unacceptable."

His face devoid of expression, Caldwell said nothing.

"You should know that Big Al Paterson fully agrees with my decision. Your successor will report for duty within days. Before then, you can expect orders for a new assignment."

He looked directly at Caldwell to make sure he had understood.

"Do you have any questions?"

Caldwell shook his head.

"Okay, then. You're dismissed. Again, I'm very sorry."

Caldwell stood, saluted, and departed without speaking.

In the span of less than a minute, Bart Caldwell's professional life had definitively and irrevocably collapsed. As an interested bystander, he had, of course, witnessed the axe falling on others, occasionally experiencing a touch of schadenfreude. That he himself would ever suffer such a fate had been unimaginable. Suddenly, he felt a need to speak with Harriet, to explain what had happened. He hoped she would understand. He hoped she would sympathize.

●

During the RCO's brief encounter with the corps commander, Tubby had waited nearby, leaning against the 16th ACR's OD sedan alongside O'Malley's aide de camp, Major Tom Crenshaw, another West Point classmate. At school, once having survived the rigors of plebe year, Crenshaw had spent the remainder of his cadet career goofing off and accumulating demerits for sundry disciplinary infractions. After graduating at the bottom of the class, he suddenly discovered a fierce urge to ascend the greasy pole of career success. His naked ambition had not endeared him to Tubby. Still, he was a classmate, so that made him fair game when it came to extracting minor favors like asking for a cigarette. If nothing else, fiddling with a smoke gave Tubby something to do with his hands.

The door to the VIP lounge opened and as quickly closed. Caldwell appeared and began slowly walking back toward the Mercedes, his head down. From the corner of his eye, he spotted Tubby and veered in his direction. Crenshaw elbowed Tubby in the ribs and nodded toward Caldwell, who was now striding directly toward them. He stopped just out of arm's reach and pointed an accusing finger at Tubby.

"Judas!" he screamed. "If the regiment is disgraced, you are the cause, Hicks!"

From the front seat of the sedan, PFC Houlihan watched bug-eyed. For his part, Tubby stared at Caldwell as if seeing him for the first time. Here, vividly displayed, was the Vietnam-induced infection that had spread such corruption throughout the upper echelons of the officer corps—the self-absorption, dishonesty, and blame shifting.

In an instant, Caldwell had made himself the embodiment of everything that Tubby had come to despise. He ground out the cigarette butt under the heel of his boot. Then, he came to attention and saluted.

"Duty, with Honor, sir!"

"Fuck you!" Caldwell replied, his face contorted with fury. "Fuck you!"

Crenshaw had grabbed Tubby's arm and was steering him toward the VIP lounge.

"You better get in and see the boss," he said.

Tubby hesitated briefly before opening the door. His hand was shaking.

Inside the lounge, General O'Malley was leafing through what appeared to be a small datebook.

"Sit down, Major. And listen up."

No time for niceties. O'Malley was all business. Tubby sat and listened attentively.

"Barton Caldwell is no longer in command of the 16th ACR. I imagine you can figure out the reason for his relief."

He glanced down at his notebook.

"Colonel Dennis Perkins will assume command. Do you know him?"

"Only by reputation, sir."

"Played for Woody Hayes at OSU, apparently. Linebacker. He'll be the first ever Black officer to command a cavalry regiment in the U.S. Army. Big Al insisted on his appointment."

O'Malley shook his head ever so slightly, as if in mild wonderment.

"Major, your job is to keep the wheels from coming off until Perkins arrives. Probably a few days. Rumor has it that, except as a skirt-chaser, your regimental XO isn't worth much. That's why I'm relying on you. Understood?"

"Yessir. Fully."

"I've read the piece coming out in the *Times*, so you can expect a lot of flak starting tonight. No way you can prevent that. Just try not to make things worse. Fixing what's broken in this outfit will be Perkins' problem, not yours."

He paused.

"Any questions?"

"Just one, sir. Yesterday, Colonel Caldwell relieved the commander of our 3rd Squadron. Does that decision stand?"

"Massey, right? Your classmate, if I'm not mistaken. God, you West Pointers are as thick as thieves. No, tell Massey that he still has his job, at least for now. I'll let Perkins decide his fate."

Crenshaw opened the door and stuck his head in.

"Sir, we've got to scoot. You and the missus are due at that Fasching event in less than two hours."

O'Malley summoned up a smile. With Ash Wednesday fast approaching, Germans were keen to let loose one last time before Lent.

"See what you get if you stay in as long as I have, Hicks? They send you to fancy dress-up balls, where you dance the night away with old ladies."

O'Malley crammed the datebook in his pocket, picked up his ballcap, and headed for the door.

"Keep that in mind as you think about your future."

"Thank you, sir. I'll be sure to do that."

●

On the ride back to Merrell Barracks, Tubby mentally ticked off all that needed to happen over the next several hours. Within the Kingdom of the

Ravens, Caldwell's removal from command would create shockwaves. Tubby needed to cushion that shock, providing assurances that an orderly transition was underway. This would require face-to-face meetings with the regimental staff and telephone calls to the several squadron commanders, Hugh Massey among them. Rumors would abound. As much as possible, Tubby needed to squelch them. The sky had not fallen.

Not least of all, he needed to drag Billy Erskine out of whosever bed he was inhabiting down in Garmisch and get him back to Nurnberg. At least nominally, Billy would command the regiment until Colonel Perkins reported. It would be helpful if he could be present for duty.

All of that promised to be relatively easy, the sort of drill that came as second nature to an experienced military officer: break down the problem into its several parts; figure out how to attack each; parcel out specific responsibilities; execute. Tubby was so accustomed to this sequence that he was oblivious to its operation. This was how the Army did things, orderly process taking precedence over purpose and imagination—and at times, obscuring their absence.

Dealing with the press fallout promised to require something more than adherence to familiar routines. If Larry Kaplan was right, the regiment could expect brutal scrutiny from several quarters.

By the time Tubby had returned to his office, the first inklings of that scrutiny had begun. In Manhattan, early editions of the Saturday *Times* were coming off the presses. Within hours, copies of the paper would be arriving in Washington. The headlines were beyond disturbing: Under the nose of a crack Army unit, the border with Communist Czechoslovakia leaked like a sieve. Corrupt G.I.s had actively abetted smuggling and shared in the loot. An endless stream of reporters would soon be pummeling the ROC with demands for an explanation: How could the Army have allowed something like this to happen? Was the explanation gross negligence, or conscious malfeasance?

By nightfall, the queries had begun. As the regiment's de facto public affairs officer, it fell to Tubby to respond. He gave priority to major U.S. newspapers, followed by American TV networks, and then to foreign news outlets, with *Stars & Stripes* last in line. To each, he offered the same basic response: While the *Times* exposé was accurate in its essentials, it lacked relevant details, namely that the commander of the 16th ACR was being reassigned and that disciplinary action against those directly implicated in criminal activity was already well underway. And with mantra-like repetition, Tubby affirmed the regiment's principled commitment to command accountability.

It was well past midnight by the time the calls stopped, allowing Tubby finally to escape from his office. Doubtless, inquiries would resume in the days ahead, with Congress sure to weigh in. For now, the press release that Tubby had hastily drafted would have to suffice as a means of keeping the sharks at bay. He directed the duty NCO at the ROC to read it verbatim to any reporter who called.

But before turning in, Tubby had one more task to undertake. Back at the BOQ, he stopped by Terry Ford's room and knocked. When no one responded, he knocked a second then a third time.

"Jesus Christ, stop! Who is it?"

The door finally opened to the maintenance officer, wearing army-issue undershirt and drawers and scratching his belly.

"Major Hicks, what the hell? Do you know what time it is, sir?"

"I do, Chief, and I'm sorry. I wouldn't have barged in, but I need a big favor, and it can't wait."

"Okay, then," Ford replied, not at all happily. "Come on in."

Ford's room was total chaos—dirty uniforms shoved in the corner and shelves cluttered with junk, to include tools and used automotive parts. The place smelled like the dorm room of a reprobate undergraduate. There was no place for anyone to sit. Not without difficulty, Tubby withheld comment.

"I'll cut to the chase, Chief. You know about the Sid Marks suicide, and I expect you know about the accident up at Rotz that preceded it."

"Of course. But what does any of that have to do with me?"

"Where is the jeep that was involved in the accident?"

"By now, it should be in the boneyard. We'll strip it for parts. Why?"

"Because the accident provided a pretext for the RCO to fire Marks—unjustifiably, in my view. I want to clear Marks' name."

"But, he's dead."

"I don't care. He's got a young daughter, and someday, she'll want to know about the circumstances leading to her father's death."

"I still don't see why that has you waking me at oh-dark thirty."

"Before it gets stripped, I'd like you to personally inspect it. Look for any signs of faulty maintenance—tires, brakes, headlights, anything. If, prior to the accident, the vehicle was good to go, then charging Marks with dereliction won't stick. And it shouldn't."

"Okay, I get it. When do you need this?"

"ASAP."

"Like today?"

"Yes, like today."

"It's now the weekend."

"Yes, I know."

"Okay, but there's something you need to know."

"What's that?"

"I was at Bon Tri."

"Huh?"

"I was B Troop's maintenance sergeant—just promoted to E-7. When I rolled into the village, there were bodies scattered everywhere."

"So, you did what?"

"My job. There was an ACAV with a thrown track. I got it moving again. Then, I left."

"So, you did not personally witness what happened?"

"Nope. But one more thing: Father Scanlan was with me. He was squadron chaplain, riding shotgun in my recovery vehicle."

"He was?"

"Yes. He always wanted to be close to the action."

"Sounds like him. Thank you, Chief. I'm further in your debt."

"You already owe me a Ravens Highball."

"No, I owe you several."

•

When he finally reached his own room, Tubby kicked off his boots, poured himself a half-tumbler of George Dickel, and dropped into his reading chair. He picked up his reading glasses and flipped open *The Quiet American*. He had reached the infinitely bleak concluding chapter, with its combination of betrayal and rough justice. After reading less than a page, he lobbed the book onto his bed. He was exhausted. Contemplating how the nation stepped off the precipice into unmitigated ruin could wait for another day.

Someone rapped on the door to his room. This late on a Friday night—Saturday morning, really—it could only be F.X.

"Come in, Padre," he commanded. "And please, help yourself to that bottle on the dresser. I'm in a mood to whine, and you're elected to listen."

F.X. poured himself a drink, sat down on the bed, and picked up the book. He peered skeptically at the cover art—an exotic rendering of Saigon in the 1950s—and let Fowler and Pyle sink to the floor. He shifted his gaze to Tubby.

"I think I know most of what you want to tell me," he said, "starting with the abrupt departure of Quickdraw Six. But I have my own sad story to get off my chest, so let me go first."

He held up his glass, as if in a toast.

"Duty, with Honor," he said, and took a swallow. "My good friend, even priests need to confess—me very much included. I need to tell you that I have been less than honest with you."

The look on F.X.'s face told Tubby to stifle any inclination to wisecrack.

"Sid Marks was telling the truth."

"What do you mean he was telling the truth?"

"I mean that troops under Hugh Massey's command were guilty of war crimes in Cambodia. What Marks said he saw happened. I was there. Or, I was there immediately after the fact.

"I know."

"You do? How?"

"Terry Ford just told me."

"I'm sorry. You should have heard it from me."

"No shit."

"All I can say is that it was horrible, Tubby."

He refilled his glass.

"I walked through the village and saw the dead—women, children, old men. Two APCs from Massey's troop were still on the scene. One had thrown a track. Terry Ford had just arrived to fix it. I asked the troops on the ground what had happened. They wouldn't even look me in the eye."

"Where was Massey?"

"Most of the unit had moved a couple clicks away. He had gone with them."

"So, you don't know for a fact that Massey himself participated."

"No, I don't. I just know that troops under his command committed crimes far worse than turning a blind eye to petty smuggling along the Czech border. And they got away with it."

"And you said nothing until just now?"

Tubby's question included evident anger.

"To my eternal shame. Those were my guys, Tubby. I was their chaplain. I couldn't bring myself to blow the whistle. So, I said nothing."

The anguish in F.X.'s voice was palpable.

"Well, goddammit," Tubby said, "what are you expecting me to do? Tell you that all is forgiven?"

"I don't know what I expect. I have no right to expect anything."

F.X. stared at the glass of whiskey gripped between his hands, and for a long moment, he said nothing. Then, he drew a deep breath.

"I only know this: Sid Marks deserved better than he got from us. For the sake of the daughter he'll never know, I'd like to see his reputation restored. And you're the only one who can do that."

F.X. stood, drained his glass, and left the room without another word. Tubby remained in his reading chair, recalling the number of times that day he had proclaimed his regiment's unwavering commitment to the principle of command responsibility.

Saturday, 21 February

The morning dawned crisp and clear. Tubby slept until past eight—an unusually late hour—and donned civvies when he finally crawled out of bed. He washed up and brushed his teeth but did not bother to shave. He was, at least nominally, off-duty.

Most Saturday mornings, the club offered a "special brunch," which was indistinguishable from breakfast served in any run-of-the-mill American café. Typically, Tubby avoided it like the plague. But, after missing dinner the night before, he was famished. A plate of bacon, eggs, and hashbrowns with toast sounded more than tolerable.

On his way to the club, he swung by the ROC. How many press inquiries had accumulated over the course of the night? Well over a dozen was the report, mostly from back in the States. The on-duty NCO-in-charge also handed him a page from a yellow legal pad containing a scribbled note. *"Major Hicks,"* it began:

> I checked the jeep, per your request. It was totaled. But I found nothing to indicate that it was not fully operational when it left Rotz. Nothing to indicate negligence. Let me know if you need anything else.
>
> Terry F.
>
> P.S. I'm taking your advice — going on leave to see my daughter and maybe my wife. So, thank you. But you still owe me that drink.

Tubby smiled, crammed the note into his pocket, and continued on to the club. He had the place almost entirely to himself. Monika was on duty and unusually cheerful as she took his order. A cup of fresh coffee allowed him to reflect on the day ahead. There would be no time for basketball with the troops. Media calls related to the border would surely resume—may have already done so. But he had decided that Sid Marks had to come first. He needed to sort things out with Hugh Massey, face-to-face, without delay.

When he settled up with Monika, he left her a larger than usual tip. She rewarded him with a smile, all the more welcome given its rarity. From the club, he returned to the BOQ, where he knocked on F.X.'s door. No answer. He proceeded directly to the regimental chapel, where he found the priest in a somber mood.

"I need your car, just for a few hours."

F.X. reached into his pants pocket, pulled out the keys, and tossed them to Tubby.

"You're going to Amberg," he said.

"I am. It's what you want me to do, right?"

"I suppose so. Mostly, I just want this entire matter off my conscience."

"Someday, you'll have to explain to me how your guilty conscience came to be my problem."

With that, Tubby pocketed the keys and left.

•

Morning traffic on the highway to Amberg was light. Tubby was guessing that, this early, the Masseys would be home.

He guessed right. When he parked F.X.'s heap in front of their quarters, the family car was sitting in the driveway. For the Masseys, a local Fasching ball the night before had become an occasion to celebrate Caldwell's firing and Hugh's restoration to command. They had stayed out late, so this morning, the house was quiet.

Tubby rang the bell. When the Massey daughters came to the door, they seemed pleased to see him.

"Good morning, Major Hicks," they said cheerfully.

"Morning, girls. I need to see your parents. Are they up?"

"We'll go see."

Together, they ran upstairs, leaving Tubby standing in the open doorway. Moments later,

Connie appeared at the upper landing. She was wearing a fuzzy pink robe that looked a bit worse for wear. As did Connie herself.

"Tubby, what in heaven's name are you doing here on a Saturday morning?"

"I've come to see Hugh, Con. It's important."

"God," she said with ill-concealed exasperation. "He's showering. Shoo the girls into the TV room and make us some coffee. I'll be right down."

Tubby did as directed. After shutting the front door, he rummaged around the kitchen for a can of coffee. He found one in the cabinet directly above an electric percolator. Calculating the number of scoops to make a pot tested Tubby's limited domestic skills. He dropped in several and hoped for the best.

By the time the coffeemaker had stopped percolating, Hugh Massey was coming downstairs, his dark hair wet and uncombed. He was wearing his standard off-duty uniform of cords and a sweater that had long since lost its shape. His feet were bare. He was in no mood to entertain visitors.

"I hope you have good reason for barging in on my family like this, Hicks."

He sat down at the kitchen table and poured himself a cup of coffee without offering any to his guest. He took a sip and made a face.

"So, what do you want? And please don't think that I'm going to thank you for getting me my job back."

"No gratitude expected, Colonel. But we have things to settle that can't wait."

Tubby took a seat facing his classmate.

"What are you talking about?" Massey demanded.

Still dressed in her robe, Connie had entered the room and was standing behind her husband. She reached for the coffeepot and poured herself a cup. She then poured a second cup, which she placed on the table in front of Tubby. He left it untouched.

"What things?" Massey again demanded.

"Sid Marks and what happened at Bon Tri, six years ago this spring."

Massey's face darkened.

"I have no interest in the late Captain Marks. Nor does anyone else, apart from that girl he knocked up."

"Maybe, but you will be interested in this: Marks wasn't lying about your unit shooting up that village, and he wasn't deluded. I have an eyewitness who will testify to what actually happened."

"So, what? God, Hicks, you're so naïve. The Army doesn't give a shit about anything that happened or didn't happen in Cambodia. Nor do most Americans. The War's over, done, forgotten. Time for you to move on. The rest of us already have."

"Not all of us. I'm going to clear Marks' name. The regiment owes him that much."

"Well, good luck trying. Do you honestly think that our new RCO will give a damn about why Marks killed himself? You may not have noticed, but I'm very good at my job. Getting off on the wrong foot with his best squadron commander will be the last thing Perkins wants to do. He needs me to succeed. So, too, does the Army, for that matter, if it's ever going to get off its ass."

Connie spoke up.

"Besides, Tubby, Hugh is one of your oldest friends!"

Tubby laughed.

"Once upon a time, perhaps. But that friendship ended long ago. Any debt I owe Hugh is long since paid in full. I'm sorry, Con."

He stood up and pushed his chair back.

"What a joke," Massey said, shaking his head. "My classmate selling me out for a dead Black guy who wasn't worth anything when he was alive."

"Duty, with Honor, Hugh," Tubby replied. "Or have you forgotten?"

Then, he turned toward the door and left.

●

It took Tubby several minutes behind the wheel to regain his composure. Massey's concluding barb had stung. How much was a "dead Black guy" actually worth? As he had grown accustomed to moving in privileged circles, Tubby had become oblivious to that question. Now, Sid Marks and Emma and Emma's child were investing it with renewed weight.

More minutes elapsed as he considered his next steps. Finally, he pulled into a roadside Esso station, where he purchased petrol for the car and a bratwurst for himself. He also used a payphone and his rudimentary German to call Nurnberg's Méridien Grand Hotel.

A clerk at the front desk answered. How can I be of help? he asked. Was a guest named Larry Kaplan still registered? Yes, he was. Please connect me to his room. On the second ring, Kaplan himself answered.

"Mr. Kaplan, this is Major Tobias Hicks."

"Major Hicks, I was just about to check out— heading back to Frankfurt. What can I do for you?"

"We should meet. Preferably, before you depart."

"A farewell drink?"

"No. Another story involving my regiment— bigger than the border scandal."

Kaplan made a sound that could suggest either interest or skepticism, or perhaps both.

"Okay, you've whet my curiosity. Meet me in the hotel bar. How long until you can get here?"

"About thirty minutes. Look for me."

It took Tubby closer to forty minutes. The day had become overcast, and it was starting to snow. Traffic in downtown Nurnberg snarled. When he pulled up to the hotel entrance, he handed the keys to an attendant accustomed to parking late-model luxury cars. F.X.'s unwashed Opel did not meet with his approval.

As promised, Larry Kaplan was waiting at the bar, nursing a cup of tea. A basket of pastries sat within easy reach.

"Care to join me?" he asked after shaking Tubby's hand.

"Yes, very much so."

Kaplan motioned to the barkeep and ordered a fresh pot.

"So, what is this hot tip that you are so eager to share with a grizzled old reporter?"

Tubby smiled. Kaplan's cynical pose amused him.

"My tip is this: Six years ago, troops commanded by then-Captain Hugh Massey massacred a group of innocent Cambodians. Sid Marks was telling the truth. I now have a second witness who will corroborate his account."

Larry Kaplan took a moment to process what he had heard. When he responded, his voice conveyed a weariness that, just moments before, had been undetectable.

"A horror, no doubt. But newsworthy? As we sit here in these very civilized surroundings, the Khmer Rouge are slaughtering hundreds, if not thousands, of innocent Cambodians on a daily basis. Our fellow citizens barely notice."

A waiter wearing a starched white jacket approached the table with a fresh pot of tea. Tubby helped himself to a cup. Saying nothing, Kaplan stared at the ceiling, as if hesitating to address a sensitive topic.

"Look," he eventually continued. "The wretched U.S. war in Vietnam has ended. For most Americans, this is cause for relief, if not celebration. Why would they want to recall a nasty incident that happened years ago?"

"Because it was a war crime, and the perpetrators—the murderers—got off scot-free."

"Well, Major, on that score, I daresay it's not exactly a unique event."

"Perhaps, but this one bears directly on what brought you here in the first place."

"Persuade me."

"This morning's *Times* tells a story of petty criminality compounded by military ineptitude. That story has troubling implications for national security. But there's another dimension that it neglects."

"Such as?"

"Race."

"I'm not following."

"A jeep accident followed by a suicide: That's what brought you to Nurnberg. The first is a common occurrence, the second tragic but not something that typically makes the front page. At the outset, the story centered on Sid Marks. By the time it appeared in print, he had all but disappeared. I think that represents a major journalistic oversight."

"You were an admirer of Captain Marks? I was not under that impression."

"Marks was no one's idea of a great soldier. But let's understand what's really going on here. The Army today is on its ass, and most Americans couldn't care less about its condition."

"I care."

"You're an exception."

Tubby picked up a packet of sugar, tore it open, and poured it into his tea.

"The point is this: The Army has a long record of tacitly tolerating racism. Now, suddenly, generals have decided that genuine equality is a precondition for repairing an institution that they themselves broke."

"Surely, you are not opposed to racial equality. Some might argue that you've been a beneficiary."

"Perhaps, I have. But I am sick and tired of people in authority royally fucking things up and then getting a pass while some nobody foots the bill. Caldwell didn't give a shit about Marks. He was *using* Marks for his own purposes."

As Tubby's voice rose, nearby patrons were taking notice. He ignored them.

"That's what this whole stinking business has driven home for me. Marks should be alive today to raise his daughter. Caldwell robbed him of that opportunity."

Tubby took a sip of tea. It was no longer hot.

"Quickdraw Six put Sid Marks in a job for which he was not qualified. He did it to show Big Al Paterson that here, in the Kingdom of the Ravens, we're all about equality. Marks thereby became a martyr sacrificed on the altar of equal opportunity."

"Very dramatically put," Kaplan said. "And you think this should interest readers of my newspaper?"

"Very much so. A volunteer force certainly *sounds* preferable to the bad old draftee Army that failed miserably in Vietnam. I get that."

"*Failed* is a harsh judgment."

"Harsh, but accurate. Of course, the conscripts themselves didn't fail. Their leaders did. And that's why Americans should think twice before buying what those same leaders are now selling. It may not be the bargain it appears at first glance."

A loud voice interrupted them.

"Aha, Tubby, I knew I'd find you here! I used Rabbi Small's Talmudic reasoning to track you down."

It was F.X., dressed in clerical garb, his Roman collar on visible display.

"Rabbi Small?" Kaplan asked, obviously mystified.

"That's Chaplain Scanlan's favorite fictional detective," Tubby answered. "Grab a chair, F.X. Your timing is impeccable. I was just explaining to Mr. Kaplan how Sid Marks ended up paying for the Army's sins in Vietnam."

"For some of them, anyway," F.X. added ruefully. "For my own sins, too."

He held up a finger to attract the waiter's attention.

"Ein bier, bitte."

Then, turning back to the table, he said:

"Notwithstanding these rags, I'm off duty."

"Then, I would like a beer, as well," Kaplan said. "And a menu."

The waiter nodded and shuffled off.

"You're causing me to miss my train, gentlemen, so I might as well make the most of it. Now, Major, back to Captain Marks. Please, explain how recounting his sad demise will enlighten the reading public. It certainly won't elicit a collective mea culpa from your Army's generals. As you rightly note, none of them have bothered to apologize for Vietnam."

"I'll settle for less than a full-fledged mea culpa. Justice for Sid Marks would do, for starters. Your paper can deliver that."

"You think so? I doubt it. The demise of Captain Marks is undoubtedly sad. But newsworthy? Not really."

The beer arrived. F.X. and Kaplan each took a long drink, and Tubby poured himself another cup of tepid tea.

"The *Times* covers stories that command national or world attention," Kaplan continued. "Smuggling along the Iron Curtain qualifies. The suicide of an obscure Army officer—whatever his color—does not. And news ages fast. I can guarantee you that, even now, Army public affairs types back in Washington are issuing press releases detailing all the actions underway to prevent further security breaches along the border."

"Most of it will be bureaucratic BS," Tubby replied.

"Perhaps, but their efforts will bear fruit. If a week from now, your regiment gets mentioned in my paper, it won't be anywhere near the front page. Some other story of the moment will claim its place."

"Your editors have a very short attention span."

"True, but consider this: The Kingdom of the Ravens may define the center of your universe, but what happens here is of no more than passing interest to the rest of us."

"Tell me what matters more."

Tubby's usual equanimity was by now long gone.

"The *Times* is an establishment paper offering an establishment perspective," Kaplan said. "If it has an overarching purpose, it's to uphold the status quo. Smooth off any rough edges, yes. Expose evildoers? Occasionally. But question the overall distribution of wealth, power, and influence? No. Without actually giving the matter much thought, my employers wish your regiment well. But, mostly, they just want you to do your job."

"That's why you're here?"

"Yes. Not to refight the Vietnam War. Not to root out war criminals or to crusade for racial justice. Just to give one small part of the Army a kick in the pants in hopes that it will finally get its act together."

"That's not good enough."

"Well, that's all I've got. That's what we do."

A noticeable chill had settled over the table.

"Now," Kaplan said, "if you choose to make the effort, I expect you could find another paper or magazine to take up your cause. How about *Rolling Stone?* It's new, and it's hot. But I have to ask: To what end? What exactly is your cause, Major?"

Kaplan picked up the menu and began to study it. Eventually, F.X. spoke.

"Tubby, Billy Erskine is back from Garmisch. He's got the ROC looking for you. Frankly, Billy could use some help."

Tubby said nothing.

"And I need my car," F.X. continued. "Zaid and I are going to the hospital to check on Emma and her baby."

"The valet has your keys," Tubby replied, his voice devoid of emotion.

"Can I give you a lift back to the kaserne? It's on our way."

"No, I'll walk. I need to reflect a bit. It's been an instructive day."

Kaplan looked up from his menu.

"I hope I did not give offense, Major."

"No offense taken. But I do need to excuse myself. I'm sure Father Scanlan is right: My friend Colonel Erskine will be needing help."

Tubby got up from his chair and shook Kaplan's hand.

"F.X.," he said, "see you back at the BOQ."

He zipped up his jacket and headed toward the lobby. By the time he reached the sidewalk outside of the Méridien Grand, he knew what he needed to do. It had come to him with startling clarity: He and the Army had reached a parting of the ways. Whatever his cause might be, he needed to find it elsewhere. He was done with soldiering.

Epilogue

The forecast was typical for Chicago on July 4th. The Bicentennial was going to be a scorcher—sunny, hot, and very humid. With Isabelle on call and expecting to be at the hospital most of the day, Toby Hicks—he had ditched his nickname upon leaving the Army—was on his own.

He welcomed the prospect of a quiet day, far from the throngs who would be crowding the Loop or Lake Shore beaches to celebrate the nation's 200th birthday. As a bonus, F.X. was passing through town, returning to Frankfurt on an evening flight out of O'Hare. Toby was eager to catch up with his friend and to show him the neighborhood that he and Izzy now called home.

They had arranged to meet at noon, on the front steps of the University of Chicago's Harper Memorial Library. Toby planned to walk F.X. through the campus where he was now enrolled, followed by lunch back at his apartment. By 3:00 p.m., he'd have F.X. in a cab bound for the United Terminal at O'Hare.

Well before noon, Toby had planted himself on a bench facing the library's handsome main entrance. To any passersby, he presented a striking figure: tall, lean, and with his head shaved. Much to Isabelle's displeasure, he had begun to experiment with growing a beard. Khaki shorts with a braided leather belt, joggers, and rimless reading glasses completed the picture of mildly iconoclastic grad-student elegance. Apart, perhaps, from the tattered gray ARMY sweatshirt that he was wearing in his friend's honor, few would mistake him for having been a professional soldier. In his lap was an old book with a tattered dustjacket.

Precisely at noon, he spotted Father Scanlan exiting a cab and lugging a bag in each hand. The priest was outfitted in wrinkled slacks and a loud, short-sleeved madras shirt that he had not bothered to tuck in. On his feet were a pair of scuffed loafers. As he mounted the stairs of the library, Toby gave a loud whistle and waved his arms. F.X. turned around and waved back. Ignoring the traffic on the busy street, he crossed quickly back to where his friend waited. Cars honked. Although not as nimble as he had once been, he managed to avoid getting run over.

Neither man was given to hugging other males, but they made an exception for each other and warmly embraced. "It's *good* to see you," they said simultaneously. "You're looking *great*," they added with less than complete sincerity. Toby could see that F.X. was putting on more weight, and F.X. was not sure if the quasi-Bohemian look worked for someone now in his thirties.

"Before I forget, Isabelle sent along a little something."

Toby handed the priest the book he had been carrying.

"She stumbled across it in a used bookstore."

It was a first edition of *The Incredulity of Father Brown* by G.K. Chesterton, published in London in 1926.

"We thought it might be entertaining, if you ever run out of Rabbi Small mysteries."

"Oh, Tubby, this is magnificent," F.X. said, genuinely taken aback. "I'm at a loss for words. Thank you."

He began to choke up.

"Okay, let's not get weepy," Toby interjected. "Time for me to show you around my new neighborhood."

He picked up the larger of F.X.'s two satchels, and they set off on a brisk tour of campus landmarks.

As they approached the imposing Rockefeller Chapel, two lanky young men jogged past.

"Hey, Toby, a bunch of us are meeting at the courts in about an hour," one of them called out. "Are you up for some ball?"

"Not today, guys. I've got out-of-town company," he said, nodding toward F.X. "Next time, for sure."

The friends entered the huge worship space. F.X. gazed appreciatively at the interior of this 20th century American knockoff of 14th century European architecture, then turned toward his friend.

"So, what's this Toby business? That's what you're called now?"

"I left Tubby behind in Nurnberg, with the Ravens."

"Probably a smart move."

F.X. laughed then gestured toward the statuary and elegant stained-glass windows.

"Your old nickname was okay for the regimental chapel," he said, "but it wouldn't work in these august surroundings."

"New life, new name, same me," Toby said with less-than-complete candor.

Several minutes later, as they approached Frank Lloyd Wright's landmark Robie House, Toby could see that F.X. was beginning to wilt. He had hoped to show his friend the home's interior, which, to his mind, possessed an authenticity that the faux-Gothic chapel lacked. But he now decided to curtail their tour.

"Tell you what," he said, "let's head over to our place. Time to get you off your feet."

F.X. nodded gratefully.

Toby and Isabelle had leased an apartment in an older three-story building on East 58th Street, just two blocks off the Midway Plaisance. Although small, it was conveniently located and represented a vast improvement over a Merrell Barracks BOQ.

As they entered the apartment, the pair dropped the bags near the door. Toby pointed to an overstuffed chair in the corner.

"Look familiar?" he asked.

With its accompanying floor lamp, it was the sole piece of furniture he had shipped home from

Nurnberg. Otherwise, the décor, from the rugs on the hardwood floors to the pictures on the walls, expressed Isabelle's feminine sensibility. Her husband was not inclined to object.

"There's the bathroom, Padre," Toby said, gesturing with a nod. "When you've finished, take a load off while I fix us lunch. Would you prefer iced tea or lemonade?"

F.X. asked for lemonade, before excusing himself to wash up. Toby went to work in the compact kitchen, located just off the living room.

"You and Isabelle have a very nice place, Tubby," F.X said as he settled back in the living room, but he immediately caught himself. "I'm sorry—I mean Toby."

"You're forgiven!" Toby said. "Now, fill me in on how you're doing, F.X. How is life at Merrell Barracks treating you?"

"I thought you knew, Toby. I'm no longer a Raven. I've been reassigned to something called the 21st Support Command, our ranks filled with warrior-clerks."

Toby snickered.

"You're a REMF!" he exclaimed. "What a hoot!"

"Well, REMFs have souls that need saving, too. And while Kaiserslautern's a long way from the front, it's not so bad. Although, I do miss Ingrid's."

"Any word on Emma back in Nurnberg?"

"I'm in touch with Zaid, and he says Emma's doing well. She and the baby live with Emma's mom."

"That might be the only good thing to come out of that entire debacle."

"Does you leaving the Army count as a good thing? Do you miss it?"

"Maybe a little. Not much."

Toby paused in thought.

"I'm not a quick study," he continued, "but, eventually, I learn. In this case, Sid Marks taught me a lot. If it weren't for poor Sid, I'd still be stuck as the longest-serving adjutant in the history of the 16th U.S. Cavalry."

"And you learned what, exactly?"

"That I was never really cut out to be a soldier. I'm not Hugh Massey, and I don't want to be. And God knows Bart Caldwell is not my idea of a role model. I'm probably more like poor old Jeff Thurlow than I would care to admit."

This thought, which had just occurred to him, Toby found oddly amusing, and it caused him to chuckle.

"So, what comes after your time here?" F.X. asked.

Toby delivered F.X. his iced lemonade, and he placed a second glass for himself on the dining-area table.

"Too soon to tell," he said. "My old tutor at Oxford pulled some strings to get me admitted here. It will take me five or six years to finish. With Izzy making good money, I've got time to figure things out. Step number one is to pick a research topic."

"Any ideas?"

"Nothing specific. But something related to the War. I'm still haunted by it."

"Well, you're hardly alone."

"Vietnam holds the master key, F.X. That's the big truth that Sid Marks helped me grasp. If we can't be honest about the War, we'll never be honest about anything—race, culture, our role in the world, whatever. And there's no way to understand the War by studying it from inside the womb. I needed to see things from the outside."

He stopped. F.X. had listened attentively, but he did not respond.

"Enough preaching," Toby said as stepped back into the kitchen before reemerging with a plate in each hand. "Let's eat."

"Happily."

Heaving himself out of his chair, the priest took a place at the table. Lunch consisted of chicken-salad sandwiches, chips, and pickles. As F.X. lifted his sandwich off its plate, Toby held up a hand, palm outward.

"Fair warning," he said solemnly. "I made the chicken salad."

The look on his face suggested more than a hint of pride. After one bite, F.X. pronounced it on a par with offerings in the Merrell Barracks officers' club. The friends laughed.

As they ate, they reminisced about people they had known in the regiment and about the Goldener Fuss. When finishing up, Toby peered at his wristwatch.

"Time for me to put you in a cab, Padre, or you'll miss your flight."

They grabbed F.X.'s suitcases and walked over to the Midway Plaisance to hail a taxi. One pulled over, and Toby tossed the two bags into its trunk. As soon as F.X. was settled in the backseat, he rolled down a window.

"I miss you, my friend."

"And I, you. More than I can say."

As the cab began pulling away from the curb, F.X. put his head through the open window.

"Duty, with Honor!" he shouted.

Toby snapped to a position of attention. To the astonishment of passing Chicagoans, he gave a crisp salute. Until the taxi disappeared into holiday traffic, he stood there, ramrod straight, without moving.

Glossary

201 ("two-oh-one") file: Individual personnel record for members of the U.S. Army

ACAV: Armored Cavalry Assault Vehicle; a modified M113 armored personnel carrier used by U.S. Army forces in Vietnam

AFN: Armed Forces Network, the television and radio service provided to U.S. military personnel and their families in Europe

ARVN: Army of the Republic of [South] Vietnam

Bavarian Border Police: state-level police organization responsible for border security within the confines of Bavaria

BGS: Bundesgrenzschutz, West German federal police organization responsible for border security

BOQ: bachelor officer quarters; housing provided not only to bachelors but to any officer traveling on temporary duty

CID: U.S. Army Criminal Investigation Division

Class VI Store: a government-operated retail outlet that sells alcoholic beverages to military personnel and their families at bargain prices.

Clicks: military slang for kilometers

CP: command post

DDR: The German Democratic Republic. i.e., East Germany

E-7: enlisted rank equivalent to sergeant first class in the U.S. Army

Fatigues: U.S. Army work uniform

Fishhook: region of Cambodia invaded by U.S. and ARVN forces in 1970

Huey: UH-1H utility helicopter

Imbiss: a German snack bar

JAG: Judge Advocate General; a military lawyer

JP-4: a blend of gasoline and kerosene used to fuel military aircraft, to include helicopters

Kaserne: a military compound or barracks

MACV: Military Assistance Command, Vietnam

NVA: North Vietnamese Army

OWC: Officers' Wives Club

Quarter-ton: military slang for the small multi-purpose wheeled jeeps widely used by the U.S. Army

RCO: regimental commander

Red Army Faction: far-left terrorist organization active in West Germany beginning in the 1970s, also known as the Baader-Meinhof Gang

REMF: rear-echelon motherfucker; Vietnam-era military slang for soldiers assigned to non-combat units

ROC ("rock"): regimental operations center

Spezi: a German soft drink blending cola and orange soda

Trace: the dividing line separating West Germany from its Warsaw Pact neighbors to the east.

TWX: communications system based on linked teletypewriters

USAREUR: U.S. Army Europe, the command that incorporated all U.S. Army units in West Germany and elsewhere on the continent

XO: executive officer

Further Reading
from the Good People at
Falling Marbles Press

FATAL FRIENDSHIP
by Stephen Paul Foster

The age-old Rousseau-Hobbes debate solved, merely requiring a grisly murder (or two)

The novel begins when Frank Bradley learns that his best friend, Rich Wahnfried, has brutally murdered his girlfriend. The ghastly news that his good friend was a closeted monster detonates Frank's confidence that he knows anyone, starting with himself.

This philosophical novel follows the path to understanding the darkness in the human condition.

THE EARLY VERSE
by Stewart Berg

A decade's worth of versified observations, collected together for the first time

Ranging from the personal to the parody and from the serious to the satirical, these poems present a decade's worth (2014-2024) of collected verse.

The companion text to this work, *The Early Prose of Stewart Berg*, is also available from Falling Marbles Press.

www.ingramcontent.com/pod-product-compliance
Lightning Source LLC
Chambersburg PA
CBHW051534260626
47170CB00003B/928

* 9 7 9 8 9 9 0 5 6 5 8 2 1 *